THE
·INTERNATIONAL·
·HOUSE·
OF DERELICTION

THE INTERNATIONAL HOUSE OF DERELICTION

Jacqueline Davies

CLARION BOOKS
An Imprint of HarperCollinsPublishers

Library of Congress Cataloging-in-Publication Data
Names: Davies, Jacqueline, 1962– author.
Title: The International House of Dereliction / Jacqueline Davies.
Description: First edition. | New York, NY : Clarion Books, [2023] |
   Audience: Ages 8–12. | Audience: Grades 4–6. | Summary: "Quirky,
   tool-wielding Alice Cannoli-Potchnik begins to repair the dilapidated
   mansion next door—only to discover the old house is home to ghosts, and
   they need mending, too"—Provided by publisher.
Identifiers: LCCN 2022022609 | ISBN 9780063258075 (hardcover)
Subjects: CYAC: Ghosts—Fiction. | Dwellings—Remodeling—Fiction. |
   Haunted houses—Fiction. | LCGFT: Novels.
Classification: LCC PZ7.D29392 In 2023 | DDC [Fic]—dc23
LC record available at https://lccn.loc.gov/2022022609

Typography by Joel Tippie
23 24 25 26 27 LBC 5 4 3 2 1

First Edition

For Lucia and Peter Gill Case,
who know what a house can mean

Chapter 1

Alice's mother owned a podium. This was not the strangest thing she owned, but it was by far the most eye-catching. The podium dominated the living room—all the other furniture seemed to bow down before it. Even the fireplace, which you would think would assert itself as the hearth of the home, crouched humbly, weighted down by dozens of framed photographs of the family on both sides. The Cannolis, Alice's mother's family, were all extraordinarily tall and thin and shaped like bendy straws with legs. The Potchniks, Alice's father's family, were all short and round and rather hairy, resembling happy bears who had eaten their fill of honey.

Alice, who was just ten and still becoming who she would

be, had gotten the best from both gene pools. She was smart and fearless, like her mother, and good-natured and a whiz at fixing things, like her father. But whether she would develop a laugh as loud as a Potchnik or learn to do a backbend like a Cannoli still remained to be seen. She was, after all, very much her own person, and as her mother often said, "Time will tell."

Alice had been home when the podium arrived. She had opened the front door and there was Dave, who worked in the college's facilities management department.

"Hiya, Alice," said Dave, leaning on the podium. "Your mom asked me to bring this over. We were about to chuck it in a dumpster, but she said to bring it here instead."

"What's wrong with it?" asked Alice, her face lighting up as she looked at the scarred and battered wood. She was a girl whose curiosity had not been dulled by too many math worksheets and required reading. Her parents believed in *unschooling*, which meant she didn't go to school; instead, *life* was school. She had her days to herself and could allow her mind to wander wherever it wanted to go. She could read or explore or experiment or daydream. In the evening, her parents would ask, with great excitement and interest, what she had learned that day, and Alice would give a detailed account of everything she had discovered: that the planets rotate around the sun and that moons rotate around the planets, that algae and fungus have a symbiotic relationship that creates lichen, that Henry David Thoreau had bought way too many nails to build his small cabin in the woods because he was such a bad carpenter. Also, that Thoreau took his laundry to his *mother's* house to get washed, so why was he considered a model of self-reliance?

"He should have put that in his book," said Alice hotly over a dinner of spicy rice and beans. "I don't think he would have sold so many copies!" Then Alice told her parents that she wanted to build a house in their backyard, and they said "Of course!" with great enthusiasm and love. But she hadn't yet found the time to do it because there was so much to learn about black holes (mysterious!) and bacteria (ubiquitous!) and the Pythagorean theorem (useful!). In fact, sometimes Alice had learned so much in one day that she still had things to tell her mother and father as they tucked her into bed and kissed her good night.

Now, with Dave on her doorstep, Alice stared greedily at the broken-down podium and knew that it would become the newest repair project for her and her father. She thought of all the things she could learn as they repaired it together: electrical engineering, chemistry, geometry, and patience.

"What's *wrong* with it?" said Dave, repeating Alice's words. "What *isn't*? I told your mom. I said, 'Professor Cannoli, the light don't work and the microphone, she's busted, and the wheels on the bottom have split clean off.' But she said, 'Dave, my husband can take anything broken and make it like new.' So here it is. Where should I put it?"

Alice pointed to the middle of the living room.

After Dave left, Alice examined the podium from top to bottom. The wiring was simple enough—Alice had rewired dozens of lamps under the supervision of her father—and she was sure she could pick up a working microphone at the secondhand surplus store that they always went to. After that, it was just a question of covering the deep scratches with wood filler, sanding it all over, staining the wood, sanding it down again, staining the wood again, applying two coats of polyurethane to make it shine, and then popping on some new wheels. Easy peasy, pumpkin pie.

By the time her father got home from his job as one of the town's building inspectors, Alice had already spread a drop cloth over the living room rug and wrestled the heavy podium into the middle of it.

"Oh, she's a beauty!" said Alice's father, running his hands along the beveled edges of the wood and smiling the famous Potchnik smile.

"I've already made a list of the things we need to do and the order we should do them in," said Alice, handing her father a piece of paper with a step-by-step plan for refinishing the podium.

"And you're feeling the Potchnik Itch, aren't you?" Whenever presented with the opportunity to fix something, both Alice and her father would feel their palms grow itchy until they picked up a tool and began the work. It was a family trait, passed down through the generations.

Alice nodded. Even the soles of her feet were itching.

Her father looked over the detailed list and nodded his head. "Alice, my little chisel, you are a smart and thorough girl. You haven't missed a thing. And I do believe you can handle this job all on your own."

"Really?" asked Alice. She'd helped her father with hundreds of household repair jobs—from plastering the walls to tiling the bathroom floor to replacing rotted beams in the ceiling—but she'd never gone solo. And now, here was her chance. To take something broken and make it like new.

"Yes," said her father, giving her one of his fuzzy bear hugs. "Besides, I've got to finish installing the new shower head upstairs so your poor mom doesn't have to squinch down whenever she rinses the shampoo out of her hair." He stepped nimbly upstairs (the Potchniks, though a stocky people, were surprisingly light on their feet), whistling as he went and tapping a beat on the banister, which he and Alice had restored when the family first moved in to this old, old house nearly a year ago.

My own project, thought Alice, looking at the podium with love. She picked up the list and headed to her father's workshop in the basement to gather the supplies she needed.

After two weeks of hard and steady work, Alice had finished the job, and the perfectly polished podium was given pride of place in the living room. And just in time, according to Alice's mother.

"Call your father, quickly!" said Professor Cannoli, sprinting in through the front door, dropping her briefcase in the hallway, and giving her daughter a ferocious hug. (Alice's mother was unusually bony, and sometimes she hugged her daughter so hard that she pressed on Alice's vagus nerve, which once caused young Alice to faint dead away.) "I have a very important lecture to deliver," Alice's mother said, hurrying to the podium. "The most important lecture of my life!"

Alice was still reeling and dizzy from her mother's hug, but she hurried to the basement stairs. *The most important lecture?* she thought. *How could it be?* Professor Cannoli had delivered so many important lectures—in her own classroom *and* the living room—how could this one be the most important of all?

Would it be more important than "The Anthropology of Modern Human Teeth as Related to Child-Rearing Practices in the Northern Hemisphere"?

Could it be more important than "An Anthropological Perspective on Utensil Use in the Cannoli-Potchnik Household"? (Conclusion: too many soup spoons, not enough teaspoons.)

Professor Cannoli's lectures were *mesmerizing*, and it was universally recognized that she was the best lecturer on campus at the small college where she taught.

"Dad!" Alice shouted from the top of the stairs. "Mom's got a new lecture!"

"Be up in a jiff!" her dad bellowed from below.

"Alice, don't yell," said her mother. "Cannolis never yell."

"But Potchniks do!" said Alice cheerfully.

"You got me there, little footnote," said her mother, rearranging her notecards. "Would you please clear the photos from the mantel and set up the projector while I make a few last-minute revisions?"

"Sure," said Alice. She moved the pictures from the mantelpiece to the coffee table, staring into the frozen eyes of family members long gone from this solid earth. Alice had heard stories about these relatives since she was old enough to sit on her parents' laps, but she often pretended not to remember so that she could hear the stories again. "Mom, who's this?" She held up a silver picture frame that contained a photo of a woman with a circle of braids around her head and a long, stiff skirt that reached to the ground.

Her mother glanced up. Even in the midst of preparing for the most important lecture of her life, she had time to tell a family story. "That's your great-great-aunt Gretel Potchnik. She was considered quite a catch in the village where she grew up, and your great-great-uncle Samuel Potchnik was lucky to get her, especially since her dowry included three goats *and* a cow. Your aunt Gretel was a terrific dancer, despite her wooden leg. And the cow was an exceptional milker, they say."

"And who's this?" Alice held up the framed picture of a tall, thin man with an enormous handlebar mustache, perfectly waxed. He was dressed in a fine suit and held a bowler hat tucked under one arm.

"That is your great-great-grandfather, Alessandro Cannoli. He stowed away on a cargo ship when he was fifteen years old, hoping to make it to America. He spent six weeks hiding in the hold of the ship with a flock of sheep. When the ship docked, he tried to sneak off, but a stevedore on the wharf spied him and shouted for others to catch the thin, dark boy hiding in the shadows. Lucky for him, no one wanted to get too close, because he'd caught a wretched disease from the sheep called *scabby mouth*, which is exactly what it sounds like. Also, he smelled horrible. Like all Cannolis, he had very long legs, so he outran them all. When he stopped running, he was in Toledo, Ohio, and he swore he would never smell that bad again. He became a very successful barber and quite a dandy, as you can tell from that picture. He actually invented a new style of mustache that was an *upside-down* handlebar. It was called the Cannoli Curl, and it was extremely popular all the way from Toledo to Cincinnati, but the fad didn't last long because it was very impractical when it came to eating hot soup."

Alice continued moving the framed photos until she pulled down the last one and was surprised to realize that her mother had never told her the story of the two girls who stared back at her. The younger one had playful eyes and a blurry half smile as if she'd been told not to move but couldn't keep herself still long enough for the photographer to take the picture. The other girl (*sisters*, thought Alice) was more serious, with strong arms, a sturdy middle, and a thick bundle of hair tied up in a bun. The expression on her face at first seemed grim, but then Alice recognized it as the grizzly-bear look of protectiveness she sometimes saw on the faces of her own parents.

Alice held up the photo and asked, "Mom?"

Alice's mother glanced up. "Oh, that's—" But then Alice's father walked into the room, and her mother asked him to draw the shades and silence his phone. Alice placed the final photo on the coffee table and quickly set up the projector so that the slides would show on the blank wall above the fireplace. Alice's mother stepped behind the podium and tapped the microphone twice so that a satisfying *thunk-thunk* echoed in the living room. Alice gave her mom a thumbs-up signal to indicate that her audio level was just right, and she and her father took their usual seats on the couch, eager to hear what Professor Cannoli would say.

Alice's mother looked straight into the eyes of her audience. "Before I begin my formal lecture, I have some news to share." Her microphoned voice filled the small room. "For the *twelfth* time since I started teaching at this college, we are being asked to *move.*"

Alice gasped. Her father leaned forward eagerly.

"As you both know, the college provides our housing as part of my compensation package. Dean Sheridan informed me this morning that we must leave this lovely home within one week's time. They have found a new house for us—as they always do. It is, I heard, an abandoned, nearly condemned structure on the northern edge of campus that the college purchased *for one dollar.* It has only half its windows. There's extensive water damage. A family of bats lives in the upstairs bathroom. I'm told the *bank* offered to *pay* the college to take it off their hands, but in the end they settled on a purchase price of one hundred pennies."

Alice's father smiled as he rubbed his great bear paws together. "No worries!" he said. "Alice and I will have it fixed up by New Year's! I could use a good project. I've nearly run out of things to fix in this house. It was some wreck when we moved in, *eh,* Alice?" He nudged his daughter with his elbow. "The exploding fuse box? The hole in your bedroom floor? The cracked bathtub and the split fixtures? What a mess! But I'd say it's about as good as it can be now."

Alice could tell by the way her father was rubbing his hands together that he was already feeling the Potchnik Itch. A whole house. There would be hundreds of repairs. That was a lot of itching.

"Remember that time we had to rewire the entire house because of the mice?" asked Mr. Potchnik.

Alice wrinkled her brow. "Was that the same house with the missing doorknobs?"

"No," said her father, "the missing doorknobs was the house with the furnace that wouldn't stay on."

"And that was the same house with the big hole in the roof, right?" Truthfully, for all her sharpness, Alice couldn't keep the houses straight. She'd lived in so many. She could remember every single repair project since she was two years old, but the houses themselves were just a blur. She had never lived one place long enough to form a solid memory of home.

"No, that—" began her father, but Professor Cannoli interrupted.

"George! We don't have time to reminisce about every house!" Alice's mother stepped out from behind the podium and sat down on the couch next to her husband. Her voice was no longer amplified by the microphone, but it was still impressive. "This is exactly the problem, George. Fixing up houses."

Alice's father's smile slipped off his face and disappeared through the floorboards that he and Alice had so carefully refinished. "Oh!" he said, and then more quietly, "Oh."

"I don't understand," said Alice, whose curious mind was capable of imagining a great many things. "Why would fixing up a house *ever* be a problem?"

"Because as long as your father continues to create beautiful homes out of these disastrous wrecks, the college will keep putting us in disastrous wrecks so that they can sell the beautiful homes he creates! For a very nice profit, by the way! Do you know how much money the college made by selling the last house we lived in? Enough to fund the Theater Arts Department for a full year!"

"I'm guessing that's a lot," said Alice's father glumly.

"Indeed!" said Alice's mother. "Although I think we can all agree that the student production of *Mamma Mia!* would have benefited from a larger costume budget!" They all nodded in silent agreement.

Alice still couldn't make sense of it. "But it's always better to take something broken and make it like new." It had been the Potchnik motto for generations. It was in their blood.

Alice's mother stood up. "This is where my formal lecture begins." She took her place behind the podium, leaned in to the microphone, and said in a low voice, "Slide number one, please."

Alice reached over to the projector and began the slideshow.

"The Anthropology of Transitional Moments and the Effects of an Erratic Upbringing on Only Children," said Alice's mother, reading the title slide. Mr. Potchnik cast his eyes down.

"Oh, Dad," whispered Alice, slipping her small hand into his large bear paw, "please don't grow melancholic. It isn't your fault."

Alice's father sighed. "I fear your mother has done first-rate research that proves otherwise."

Chapter 2

Alice's father could not have been more correct.

"And so, in conclusion," said Professor Cannoli, eighty-three slides later, "taking into consideration the special emotional requirements of children without siblings, the structural stresses that families face when moving from one house to another, and the importance of a sense of rootedness and grounding in children, particularly during the critical ages of *nine to twelve*, we see that stability and continuity are crucial to the development of a personality that is vigorous, self-confident, and resilient, as opposed to one that is marked by hopelessness and *indistinct unhappiness*."

"But, Mom," said Alice, not even waiting to raise her hand,

"I don't feel hopeless or even a little bit unhappy. I think I'm fine."

"Of course, you are, strudel," Alice's mother responded. "You're more than fine. You're delightful and intelligent and winsome and brave and bursting with curiosity and creative energy. But you can't ignore science! If we keep moving from house to house, it's only a matter of time before you turn. The data is unusually strong."

Alice thought about a peculiarity she'd never told her parents: When she slept deeply and dreamed that she was home, she never dreamed of any *particular* house. The space she dreamed of was nothing more than empty rooms through which she wandered, rooms without furniture or features or details of any kind. She had lived in so many houses that her dreams declared she had lived nowhere.

Still, Alice wasn't convinced. "But I have both of you. I don't need a place to call home. Wherever we go, *that's* home. And it doesn't matter how many times we move, as long as we're together."

Professor Cannoli's eyes shone in a way that said to her daughter, *You are the light of my life.* "Oh, Alice," she said, "that's such a beautiful sentiment. Unfortunately, it's complete hooey. Children your age need a sense of stability and permanence, and that is most often rooted in a place—a stable home. The science is clear. We must stop all this moving about."

Alice's father slumped on the couch. Alice's mother once

again left the podium and sat down next to her husband.

"George. You are my love, and nothing will ever change that. But we must stop this endless uprooting. For the sake of our child, our only child, our *Alice*." She rested her head on his shoulder, which required all of her Cannoli bendiness, because she was so much taller than he was.

Alice's father looked at his hands, resting idly on his knees. "Are you saying we'll refuse to move?"

"That we cannot do. Unfortunately. It's in my contract, clear as day: the college can move us anytime it sees fit. *But*— we can make sure this is the *last* move. Which means that you, heart of my heart, must make the greatest sacrifice of all. *You must not fix up the next house we move in to!*"

Alice's father blinked his eyes. "You mean unless something is broken."

"Not even then," said Alice's mother gently.

"But if there's a cracked windowpane—"

"You leave it cracked."

"But if there's a creaky floorboard—"

"You let it creak."

"Surely, if a faucet is dripping—"

"Then *drip, drip, drip*," said Alice's mother. "We will live in that house as it falls down around our ears until Dean Sheridan understands that we will not be moved around like pieces on a chessboard. Until the college agrees to give us the next house to be our forever home, we will not be budged!"

"I don't know if I can," said Alice's father. "Chipped

tilework must be replaced. Dirty walls must be painted. A rotten porch must be—"

"Left alone," said Alice's mother firmly. *For Alice.*

Alice's father looked at his daughter and nodded. "For Alice. The most important thing in our lives."

His eyes began to fill with tears. Alice's mother began to well up, too.

"George, sweetheart," she warned, "if *you* begin to cry, then *I* will begin to cry, and if I begin to cry, you will cry even harder. And I ask you: How will it end? We will be swept away by our tears, and then who will take care of Alice?"

They both looked at their daughter with such tenderness that it would have made any ten-year-old burst into tears on the spot. But Alice, dry-eyed and clear-minded, was not any ten-year-old. She was a rare old soul with more flint and steel in her small body than most people might have guessed.

"How is it possible to let a dripping faucet *keep dripping*?" Alice asked. The idea was ridiculous. Like expecting a fish to fly or deciding to chuck an old podium in a dumpster. It wasn't the Cannoli-Potchnik way.

"I don't know, little cabbage," said her father. "But we're going to find out. Together. We will lay down our tools and take a vow of not-fixing. In fact, I will make a Cannoli-Potchnik Oath."

Alice's eyes grew wide. The Cannoli-Potchnik Oath was sacred in their family, having been handed down and adapted, in various forms, through generations on both sides. It was used in only the most serious situations.

Alice's father stood and faced Alice and her mother. He made fists out of both hands and crossed them at the wrists in front of his chest. "I take this solemn Cannoli-Potchnik Oath: I will not repair *anything*, no matter how broken it is, until we are given our own forever home." He then advanced his fists, still crossed at the wrists, and extended his right leg, as if presenting both a shield and a sword on a great battlefield.

Alice's mother hugged Alice and then her husband fiercely with her bony arms. "And now, we pack!" she announced. "Alice, darling, please put all the framed photographs in a box and label it 'Do Not Discard.' Remember, those pictures are the most prized possessions we own. As I've often said—"

"If we don't remember our ancestors," recited Alice, "who will remember us?"

"Well quoted, my little citation! George, darling, bring down the packing boxes, please and thank you. I'm going to start sorting through the utensil drawer. My research has certainly shown we don't need all the soup spoons we own! I do believe it's time for a Cannoli-Potchnik garage sale!"

Garage sales were as much a part of life in the Cannoli-Potchnik household as moving, lecturing, and fixing up. Alice and her parents had it down to a science.

Step one: Gather up everything you can bear to part with. (For Alice and her parents, this included nearly everything, because they weren't particularly attached to stuff. They cared much more about people and history and ideas and honest work.)

Step two: Have a garage sale and price everything so ridiculously low that absolutely every item sells.

Step three: Use the profit from the sale to go out for a celebratory dinner at the Olive Garden. (Because it was a celebration, Alice would get *two* desserts and her parents would share a glass of wine.)

Step four: Pack up whatever is left, attempting to set a family record for moving a household with the fewest number of boxes.

Step five: Haul the boxes to the new house. (While the Cannoli-Potchniks didn't own a car, they had six red wagons precisely for this purpose, and Dave always delivered their furniture in a truck.)

Step six: Once you're settled in your new house, buy all the things you now realize that you *do* need, like reading lamps and egg cups and ice skates and terrariums. (Alice's family accomplished this step by going to neighborhood garage sales, often buying back the exact items they had just sold.)

And that's how the Cannoli-Potchniks did garage sales.

Alice was packing the family photos and thinking about what her mother had said. She was certain that her mother's hypothesis was wrong. In fact, Alice believed the opposite was true. She considered her ability to pack up and leave without dragging so much as a memory of the house with her to be one of her superpowers. It made her flexible and unencumbered, as light as a feather that blew in the wind. Adaptable.

After all, in Alice's experience, houses were places you

fixed and places you left. Moving every few months was good practice. It taught you not to count on things that might not be there when you needed them. Who needed a permanent home? Not her.

As Alice packed the framed photos, she found that the extra-large box she was filling was not big enough. No matter how she arranged and rearranged, the pictures wouldn't all fit. Did she *need* to pack them all? She looked at the one of the two girls she didn't know, which was in a particularly beautiful antique silver frame. Alice was sure they could sell that frame at the garage sale for a good price. That would cover her extra dessert! "Do we need *all* the photos?" Alice shouted to her mother.

"All!" came the answer from the kitchen.

Alice had known this would be her mother's response, but there was no more room in the box! Would it be *so* terrible to let one photograph go? She held it in her hand and stared at the girls. *I don't even know you*, she thought.

But in the end, she applied several mathematical formulas related to area and volume and did fit all the pictures, knowing that she would lug the box to the new house and then struggle to find room for the framed photographs on the new mantelpiece. What's old becomes new, just as things that are new will always grow old.

It was their most successful garage sale ever. In fact, even after their Olive Garden feast, there was a tidy sum of money left over. Alice's parents gave it all to Alice, telling her to spend it on something that filled her with joy, enlightened her mind, and made the world a better place. (Her parents often talked poetically after a celebration at the Olive Garden.)

The next day, as the sun was dipping below the horizon, they pulled their six wagons across campus to move in to their new old house. Luckily, Professor Cannoli had a map because their new address was in an unfamiliar neighborhood, at the end of a dead-end street, obscured by blackthorn bushes that had grown to a frightening height.

"Wowza," said Alice's mother, staring at the crumbling brick house in front of them. An eight-foot-high wall enclosed the entire backyard, as if it were a prison with the house standing guard.

"Holy Cannoli," whispered Alice's father, looking queasy as he stared at the broken windows, the sagging roof, and the front door hanging on a single hinge.

Alice said nothing. She was looking at the house next door. A breeze had gently lifted her hair and blown it in that direction, and now she couldn't take her eyes off the stately dark house that hulked in the dimming light. It was as if some unknown force was beckoning.

Alice's mother led the way inside their new home, followed closely by Alice's father. But Alice let go of the wagon handles and wandered into the adjoining yard. She was accustomed to going where her curiosity led her.

There was a large wooden sign in front of the dilapidated

mansion, one of the familiar green-and-white signs that marked every building owned by the college. The sign was overgrown with stubborn ivy and brittle mugwort, and the lawn was choked with wilted dandelions. Alice had to rip away at the plants to reveal the writing on the sign.

By the time she could make out the words, the light was dim indeed. Written in ordinary block lettering was INTER-NATIONAL HOUSE. But below the official lettering, in words scrawled by hand, she read OF DERELICTION.

Chapter 3

The Cannoli-Potchnik family stuck to their resolution.

They covered the broken windows with thick sheets of plastic, boarded up the holes in the floor with plywood, and stuffed steel wool into every crumbling crack they could find.

But they did not *fix* anything.

They adapted. They got used to taking icy showers and cooking on a hot plate and carrying flashlights from room to room. In the evenings, they snuggled together on the couch under several quilts and read books or played card games or quizzed each other on ancient Greek myths. Sometimes they stopped to sing songs as loudly as they could in an effort to drown out the deafening noise of the ancient heating system.

It clanged and bellowed like a herd of bison wearing cowbells, but it never seemed to kick up much heat.

It was September, with the crisp fall air that September brings and a new school year beginning. Because the house was on the very edge of campus, Alice's mom had a much longer walk to her office in the Department of Anthropology, but her pipe-cleaner legs carried her quickly where she needed to go. Alice's father, on the other hand, was now closer to a bus stop that took him directly to the town offices every day.

As for Alice, the only thing that mattered to her was her proximity to the college library. From there, she could learn about any subject of interest. At the moment, she had checked out a colossal library book called *Images of American Living: Three Centuries of Domestic Architecture*. Alice had been studying the craft of tilework in historical homes, and the book was filled with glossy photographs of houses, inside and out.

"What will you study today, Alice-noodle?" asked her mother as she stuffed papers, her laptop, and the delicate skull of a Burmese python into her briefcase.

"I'm going to explore the neighborhood," said Alice. "I don't know this part of campus."

"The *northern* edge of campus," said Professor Cannoli, with a flick of her wrist that showed her displeasure. "Where the Mathematics Department holds sway. And *Computer Science!*" Professor Cannoli had a simmering feud with the Computer Science Department. She felt they had cheated during last year's faculty volleyball game, which the Social Sciences had lost to the Engineering Department by a single point.

Alice's father bounced into the room, late to catch his bus. "I love you both," he said as he kissed his daughter and wife.

"As do I!" sang Alice's mother, giving her daughter a ferocious and heartfelt hug that left Alice pale and wobbly in the knees.

As soon as her parents left, Alice wandered out the front door and over to the wooden sign in front of the neighboring house. The creeping plants that she had torn away so vigorously the day before had grown back. They covered the sign with their twisting vines and dangerous barbs as if reclaiming it for their own. Through the foliage, Alice could see that one of the signposts was nearly rotted through. Rust spots bloomed around the corroded nails hammered into the splintered wood. Alice pushed away the leaves and nettles to look at the handwritten words OF DERELICTION. She wondered who had written them and what they meant.

Alice glanced in the direction of the front door and saw a cardboard notice taped to it.

The orange sign with its bold black lettering seemed to shout at her.

"I get it," she muttered.

Alice knew what "condemned" meant; her father was, after all, a building inspector. She also knew that demolitions were hard to schedule, which was probably why the date on the sign was left blank. You had to get permits from a lot of different departments, and there were almost always people who protested the tearing-down of old buildings, especially if they were examples of important styles of architecture.

Alice's curiosity was instantly engaged. Was this an example of an important style of architecture? She ran next door to her house and retrieved the heavy library book. Sitting cross-legged under the giant sycamore tree in the front yard of the condemned building, she turned the pages of the book until she found a photograph that was nearly a perfect match.

The house was an excellent example of Georgian architecture, which meant it was probably more than two hundred years old. It had a rigidly symmetric façade made of pale stone, double-hung windows with twelve panes each, and a paneled front door framed by four large columns with a curved pediment on top. The roof sloped on all four sides, which Alice learned was called a hip roof, and there was a single prominent window (called an eyebrow dormer) centered on the front slope. The window did in fact look like a giant eye keeping a close watch on the street below.

Alice stared at that eye. A breeze lifted her hair as it had the day before, causing it to flutter around her shoulders. She took a sharp breath in, then whispered "Hello" on the exhale.

The sun, glancing off the glass of the single-eye window, glinted, as if the house had winked at her.

Or perhaps it was inviting her inside?

Alice knew full well that no one was supposed to enter a condemned building. There were all kinds of dangers. There might be hazardous materials, like broken glass or black mold or unsafe chemicals. Often, there were infestations of disease-ridden pests. Once in a while, live electrical wires were exposed. Beams could fall, stairways crumble, and floorboards give way. The greatest danger, however, was that the entire structure might collapse at any moment, burying alive any hapless wanderer who had ventured inside. And how could you ever be found if you hadn't told anyone where you were?

Condemned houses were strictly off-limits, and especially so if you were the daughter of one of the town's building inspectors.

Alice closed the library book and stowed it safely under the front steps of her own rotting porch. Then she returned to the old mansion, noting the date engraved in the corner-stone: 1785. This was a house that had stood for hundreds of years. The stonework along the foundation seemed level and well seated, and Alice could see that the house rested on a stone cellar, which was a good sign of stability. She kicked at the foundation, as her father had taught her to do. Nothing wobbled or fell from the wall. From her pocket she retrieved the all-purpose tool that she carried with her, opened the screwdriver attachment, and used it to poke at the wooden windowsills, as she had seen her father do on many occasions when she accompanied him to work. The sills were badly rotted, and many of the windowpanes were cracked or broken, but none of the framework had shifted or was out of plumb. The stonework was solid, even if the wood on the outside could be chipped away by a curious ten-year-old.

Alice pressed the open palm of her hand against the stone wall, then pulled it away in surprise. The wall was in shade, but the stone was warm like a loaf of bread out of an oven. What could possibly warm the house from the inside?

Alice placed her palm on the wall again and let it rest there. Was it her imagination or did she feel a vibration? Or perhaps a beating, like a drum. Steady. Calm. Regular. She stood still, listening in the silence, but there was no sound, only the feeling on her skin and in her blood vessels. It took her a minute to realize that the beating was in synchrony with her own heartbeat. *Oh, it's just me!* she thought, feeling ridiculous, as if the house had played a joke on her. No doubt the pulse in her wrist was causing her palm to sense a rhythm. And perhaps the warmth she felt was really just in contrast to her own cool hands.

She walked around the house again, this time paying attention to the bulkhead door that led to the cellar. The door was locked with a rusted padlock, but when Alice yanked on the wooden handle, the whole thing came off in her hands.

Another invitation? It was as if the house were saying to Alice, *It's about time you showed up.*

The door opened onto a coal chute. Alice flicked on the flashlight that came with her all-purpose tool and shined the light down the dark hole. She could see clear to the floor of the cellar. The distance was no more than seven feet, so she slipped her legs into the small opening and lowered herself down the chute, dropping the last three feet into the empty coal bin. She scrambled over the wooden side, feeling a splinter pierce the flesh of her index finger.

"Ow," she said as she landed with a gentle thud on the soft, dirt floor.

The cellar was dark. Alice stretched her index finger into the shaft of light that fell through the open bulkhead door and used the tweezers from her utility tool to pull the thick splinter from under her skin. A single drop of blood, ruby red and thick, welled up from the spot and fell from her finger. When it hit the sandy, dry floor, it disappeared, as if swallowed up by the house itself. Alice bent down and shined her flashlight beam where the red droplet had landed, but there wasn't so much as a mark to show that blood had been spilled.

Alice put her tool in her pocket and looked around. In the dim light, she could see the octopus arms of an ancient coal-burning furnace and the stairs that led to the first floor of the house. The rest of the cellar was bare, except for the wooden stalls along one wall that had once held all manner of things needed to run a house of this size: chopped wood, blocks of ice, root vegetables, coal. Alice poked her head into a few of the bins, but they were empty.

The air in the basement was cool and slightly damp, but not musty. As she stood still, Alice could again feel a steady heartbeat, this time through the soles of her feet. She knelt down and put both palms on the smooth floor. A spider dropped down on a thin strand of silk and dangled in front of her face, seeming to watch her. Alice held her breath, feeling the pulsing in her hands, and now she knew: This heartbeat wasn't her own.

"Hello?" she whispered again. But the house didn't respond. The spider quickly retreated up the silk path it had spun.

When Alice opened the door at the top of the cellar stairs and emerged into the foyer of the house, she was nearly blinded. Light gushed through the eight-foot-high windows that lined the front of the house, spilling into the entryway and tumbling into the front parlor. It bounced up the mahogany staircase that curved gracefully to the second floor and danced around the hundreds of crystals in the extravagant chandelier that hung crookedly above Alice's head.

But what the light illuminated, more than anything else, was the utter ruination of the house.

Decay, deterioration, and neglect marked every inch of the once-grand residence. The ceiling was streaked with ugly brown stains from a broken water pipe on the second floor.

The decorative plasterwork that ran along the edges of the ceiling had fallen off in great chunks. Pieces of it lay smashed and scattered across the foyer tiles. The floor-to-ceiling windows rattled as draft after draft blew through the old house.

Everywhere, there were the forgotten remains of lives once lived in this place: a stack of moldering newspapers, a battered chair with a missing leg, a wooden crate filled with broken dishes, dust-covered drapes left hanging over the banister, a faded photograph album filled with tattered portraits of people who had long been forgotten.

Alice felt as though her heart would break in two, splintering like the house itself. A proud house that had once been the home of children as they grew into adults, and adults as they journeyed to old age, and old people as they departed this life now lay in ruin, and no human on earth—not even a Potchnik—could fix it.

"Oh, House," she whispered. "I wish I could do something."

A sound like the beating of wings drew her attention to the front parlor. She stepped into the room, which was empty except for a faded sofa, and heard the gentle chirring of birds as they settled. Alice shined her flashlight up the flue, and a flock of chimney swifts took flight at the sudden brightness, flying up and away. As she moved back from the fireplace, her foot stepped on a loose floorboard that squeaked like a mouse.

Alice looked around the room. Her eyes landed on the fireplace, surrounded by tile. Almost half the original tiles were missing completely, but the dozen that remained were Delft tiles, blue and white with pictures of everyday life in Holland: a boat sailing on an ocean, a windmill turning in a breeze, a cow lying in a pasture.

The tiles were all broken, except for one—the heart tile, which was centered directly over the hearth. It showed a young girl about Alice's age carrying a large basket on her hip that overflowed with tulips. Alice liked this tile; it gave her a feeling of hope. She touched it with her five fingertips.

Often her father had told her *a fireplace is the heart of a home*. But this heart was cold, the tile cool and flat. It had been many years since there'd been a fire to warm the heart of this house. Alice looked around for something that could bring warmth, something that could revive.

After carefully checking to make sure that the chimney was clear, she gathered scraps of wood from the floor. She leaned the bits of wood against a crumpled piece of newspaper, then used the flint in her utility tool to create a spark, just as her parents had taught her. The old newspaper caught fire immediately. Alice knew the flames would burn for only a few minutes, but she hoped it would help to dispel the feelings of neglect and abandonment that seemed to drip from the mildewy walls of the house.

The fire burned cheerfully. Alice looked again at the tiles, then used her hand—thumb and pinkie outstretched the way her father had taught her—to make some rough measurements. Originally, the fireplace had been surrounded by twenty-one of these Delft tiles, each one six inches square. It was a shame so many of the tiles were broken, and so many missing altogether.

"I wish only one tile was broken," Alice said aloud, as if talking to the house. "I could fix just *one*." And then she remembered something her father had said to her when they were stripping and sanding the twenty-seven balusters on the staircase in their last house. She had said, "I can do *one*. But I can't do all twenty-seven!" Her father had said, "If you can do one, then you can do two. If you can do two, then you can do four. If you can do four, then you can do eight. When you think about it, there really isn't anything you *can't* do. The question is, *do you want it enough?*"

Alice looked at the girl with the basket of tulips, and thought silently, *I want this*.

Chapter 4

Alice used the last clean corner of her rag to polish the final new tile. She had found twenty replacement tiles from the salvage shop, and now all twenty-one tiles were in place, neatly framed by the old wooden mantel of the fireplace. The mortar had set; the grout was dry. It was "a job well done," as her father would have said. A job that any Potchnik could be proud of.

Alice rocked back on her heels and sighed with satisfaction. She had taken this one thing, this one most important thing in the House—for everyone knows that the fireplace is the heart of any house—and fixed something broken and made it like new. There was no better feeling in the world.

A draft blew through the room, and Alice felt as though the House was sighing with her. The breeze sounded like a long, satisfied *ahhhhhh* now that the fireplace was returned to its original state of grace. It had been only three days since she first entered the House, but she already felt a closeness to it, as if they had spent the days in easy conversation, getting to know one another. That's how it was when you were fixing something: a slow acquaintance between you and the object.

She turned to look at the tall windows that let in such gusty bursts of air. Something caught her eye. A shimmer. A reflection. A refraction. The light seemed to change directions, to dance. Alice stared at the space. It looked as though the light that spilled in through the window was in motion; it appeared to advance and then retreat, flowing in and out of different shapes, blooming and then dying like a flower whose season has passed.

Alice closed her eyes. When she opened them again, all she saw was the bright sunlight, falling in steady beams through the glass and onto the floor.

But then there it was again! Over by the archway. And then next to the sofa. Alice followed the flowing patch of light as it bounced around the room, restless, agitated, unable to settle in any one spot until it reached the fireplace. There, it seemed to coalesce, to become more solid—if such a thing could be said of light. The ebbing and flowing energy hovered in front of the fireplace, not more than three feet from Alice, gently bobbing up and down as if it were a rowboat on a quiet sea.

"What are you?" Alice whispered.

The light swirled, briefly spinning out luminescent petals, then settled again, and Alice had the strange sense that it was *looking* at her. She kneeled down and slowly reached her hand forward.

Something crashed upstairs, far away. The sound was muffled, but there was no missing that distinct quality of destructiveness. Startled, Alice dropped her hand and turned to look up the great staircase. When she turned back, the patch of light had disappeared. Instead, she was staring into the ceramic eyes of the little Dutch girl, forever carrying her basket of tulips.

"Mom," Alice said that evening. "I'd like to get my eyes examined."

"Well, of course, if you like. But the Cannolis *and* the Potchniks have outstanding vision. We always have. Grandmother Cannoli could shoot a quarter out of the sky, even when the sun was shining right in her eyes, and your great-great-"—she paused, counting off the number of "greats" by tapping her fingers—"great-uncle Ivan is famous for having spotted the czar's troops advancing on his tiny village in the middle of the night when there was no moon at all."

"I'm having the opposite problem," said Alice. "I'm seeing things that *aren't* there."

"Oh, my! That must be very unsettling," said her mother. "But interesting! You know, in some cultures, visions are—" She caught herself about to deliver a lecture. "I'm sorry, sweet pea. By all means, stop by Health Services tomorrow, and please say hello to Dr. Lupia for me. You can tell her my rash is all cleared up. Huzzah!"

But the next day, Alice decided to do an eye test of her own. She filled her canvas tool bag with sandpaper, wood filler, a tack cloth, and her work gloves, along with all the regular tools she often used, and returned to the International House of Dereliction. Now that the Delft tiles looked so perfect, Alice knew she needed to restore the wooden mantelpiece that surrounded them. It wouldn't do to have those beautiful tiles showcased by a mantel that was gouged and splintered.

It was a gloomy day with heavy dark clouds that refused to rain out of spite. The kind of weather that tended to scatter Alice's thoughts and make her feel less hopeful than she usually did.

She slipped out the front door of her own house. The back door was essentially useless because it opened onto the walled garden, enclosed all around by brick. There were no gates or openings of any kind, but it wouldn't have mattered if there were: the garden was so radically overgrown and untended, it had become as impenetrable as the deepest forests of the Amazon.

In fact, on the first day in their new house, the Cannoli-Potchniks had looked out on the walled garden with its vicious tangle of plants and vowed never to set foot in it. "We are not blessed with green thumbs," said Professor Cannoli, closing the door and turning the lock. "Neither the Cannolis nor the Potchniks. In fact, back in the seventeenth century, a direct ancestor of mine was strangled to death by a vining clematis."

It was agreed all around: They would leave the garden wild and undisturbed.

This morning, Alice crossed the neighboring yard diagonally and entered through the back door of the House. The front entrance of the condemned House was too exposed.

Upon arriving, Alice became distracted by the chandelier that hung from the ceiling in the parlor. A cut-glass pendant had fallen since yesterday and lay broken on the floor. Alice scouted around and found a broom and a dust bin, but when she returned to the parlor, another pendant had come loose and fallen. They were dropping like teeth out of an old person's mouth.

Alice didn't want to spend the day sweeping up broken bits of glass, so she went home and carried a work ladder over to the House. Upon examination, she counted twenty pendants that were missing.

In Alice's opinion, one of the best things about living on a college campus was that things were close by. Professors' offices and shops, health services and libraries, dining halls and post offices—nothing was more than a bike ride away. Alice was very accustomed to riding her second-hand Raleigh with a milk crate lashed to its back to transport whatever she needed.

She pedaled over to one of the restoration/junk shops that she and her father haunted and showed the owner, Rose, the samples of pendants she had taken from the chandelier. They spent a pleasant hour sorting through a large cardboard box filled with salvaged cut-glass pieces of all shapes and sizes, chatting about Rose's three cats and baseball and the difference between a royal flush and a full house, until they had found enough good matches for Alice's chandelier. Alice was thankful to have the heap of money left over from the garage sale. Even after buying the Delft tiles from the salvage shop, she still had plenty, and Rose gave her an extra good price on the pendants. They were, after all, just forgotten bits of glass that no one wanted. Alice pedaled off with what she needed tucked safely in her milk crate, including a box of candles that Rose had given her for free.

The Rule of Potchnik! her father would have shouted joyfully as Alice worked on the chandelier. Today, that rule would have been: *Estimate that any project you begin will take three times as long as you expect!*

The Rule of Potchnik, however, changed from day to

day, depending on the job at hand. Sometimes, the Rule of Potchnik was *Measure twice, cut once*, which meant, *Take the time to plan carefully so you don't make mistakes that can't be fixed.*

Sometimes, the Rule of Potchnik was *The right tool for the right job*, which meant, *Don't try to get away with using whatever you have on hand because you're too lazy to get the tool you really need.*

Some days, the rule was *Never give up*, but other days, it was *Know when to quit.* It wasn't easy following the Rule of Potchnik.

Alice had spent the day ping-ponging between these last two interpretations of the rule: She was determined to finish the chandelier, but she had discovered that the entire thing needed to be restrung. She felt utterly discouraged as hour after hour passed. What had begun as a simple patch-and-fill job turned into a complete overhaul. As it often did.

But after six hours of concentrated work, the chandelier was restored and Alice was ready to place the ten tapered candles into their original holders. The chandelier had, of course, been wired for electricity at some point over the years, but there was no power in the house, and Alice was thankful the original candleholders had been left in place.

She climbed the ladder and used her flint tool to light the first candle, then used that candle to light the others, carefully turning the circle of the chandelier to reach all around. When the last candle was lit, she let go. The chandelier unwound itself, spinning like a carousel, all ten candles aflame and the hundreds of glass pendants sparkling like diamonds under a generous sun.

Oh, how beautiful! a voice whispered.

Chapter 5

Alice nearly fell off the ladder, but managed to hang on as she looked around the empty room. Had it been a voice, or had it been . . . bells? But bells didn't make words! And had she really "heard" anything at all? To Alice, it seemed as if the sound, whatever it had been, had entered through her *skin*, skipping her ears entirely and sinking straight into her bones and organs.

"Who said that?" asked Alice.

There was silence, and then Alice sensed a vibration in her rib cage that she felt as the words: *You can hear me?*

"Yes, I can hear you," said Alice, looking around the room. "Except . . ." She paused. "I'm not really *hearing* you. I'm feeling what you're saying. I'm feeling the words . . . in my bones and muscles."

Alice looked around the room and saw the wavering patch of light she had seen yesterday, hovering near the chandelier. This time, she could make out faint colors in the wavelengths of light—soft blues, forest greens, and the palest of yellows.

Jeepers! There was a long pause, and Alice held her breath. *You must have received the Blessing of the House. You're the first! I've never known a living human who was given the Blessing of the House.*

"The *what?*" Alice's years of unschooling had taught her that things are not always what they seem, which is to say she was more prepared than most to converse with a voice that couldn't be heard as it radiated from a patch of light in a house that was condemned.

The Blessing of the House. There was a pause. *Jiminy! You must have done something awful special.*

"But I haven't," said Alice. Her truthfulness came from both the Cannolis and the Potchniks and was perhaps the one family trait that could never be changed.

The patch of light darted to the fireplace, moving so quickly that Alice lost sight of it for a moment. Suddenly, her skin tingled all over as if she were swimming in a pool filled with carbonated soda. Immediately she knew that the patch of light was laughing.

You sure did! You fixed the House's heart! The patch of light swirled and flew up to the chandelier, which it circled. *And today you made everything sparkle. I think the House is saying 'thanks very much!'* Again, Alice felt the giddy tickling of thousands of invisible bubbles dancing on the surface of her skin.

Alice looked around. A house that was alive? She thought of the heartbeat and the unexpected warmth in the walls. She thought of her blood disappearing without a trace into the floor of the basement.

"Can you see me?" asked Alice.

The voice laughed. Alice imagined sleigh bells jingling up and down her spine. *Of course I can see* you. *You're a living human. You're so . . . fleshy.*

Alice was puzzled by this comment. "What do you mean, 'a living human'? What are you?"

I'm—

Silence! Reckless child! Alice's insides began to rumble and churn as if all her internal organs were slowly tumbling in a cement mixer. Someone else had entered the room. Where? Alice looked around the parlor until she noticed a second patch of light hovering under the archway of the foyer.

She could be a traitor, growled the stony-hard voice. *They come in all disguises.*

Alice stared closely at the patch of light, noticing how different it was from the first. This white-hot light was all sharp angles and angry edges. It looked like a mirror that had splintered into a hundred pieces, and the pieces were constantly rearranging themselves, agitated and dissatisfied. They moved close together, almost forming a complete surface but not quite, before shattering and falling and then beginning again to recompose.

We must be on our guard. Spies. Turncoats. They look like us, you know! Alice felt the vibrations of this voice all the way to her bones—a crunching, rasping, grating feeling that made Alice want to grind her own teeth to push the sound out of her skull.

Oh, shush, you, said the voice that sounded like bells. *You always spoil the fun. I haven't talked to anyone in ages!*

An argument commenced. Alice's guts tumbled inside her, while her skin tingled as if snow were falling on it.

You are the most stubborn child—

Stop being a cranky-pants!

You will lead us to ruin!

Oh, as if! You're such a fuddy-duddy!

Insolent!

Doodle bug!

"Stop!" shouted Alice. "My insides!"

There was silence, and the tingling and churning ended abruptly.

The silver bells spoke first: *My name is Ivy. And this is Mugwort. We both died in the House . . . obviously. Not at the same time, though. Mugwort had been here for ages before me. He actually built the House. We think. We're not sure, but we think he did.*

The bells jangled up and down as if someone were playing chaotic scales on a piano. Alice sensed that Ivy was nervous, and her anxiety made Alice feel calm by contrast.

"Why aren't you sure?" Alice asked. It seemed to her to be a very strange thing not to know if you had built a house.

Oh, it was so long ago! Ivy jingled. *I mean, just forever ago. And we forget things. It's the way, you know. Or maybe you don't? I can't remember what it was like before. Did I know that I would forget everything?*

"What *everything*?"

The tinkling response of the bells was so quiet, Alice could barely hear: *Everything.*

Suddenly Alice's insides heaved, and a tremendous booming like the firing of a cannon rattled her bones: *WE FOUGHT AND WON AT THE BATTLE OF SARATOGA. WE LOST WITH HONOR AT THE BATTLE OF BRANDYWINE—*

Mugwort, we know! Stop it! You're making her sick. Alice had never heard bells ring so furiously. Mugwort fell silent, and Alice's kidneys settled into their proper places.

"So," said Alice drawing out the word to give her more time to consider how to phrase her question. "You're dead. You're . . . ghosts?"

Oh no! Don't— began Ivy, but before she could finish, Alice was shaken all the way to the marrow of her bones, as if a thousand stones were hailing down from the sky.

Mugwort! She didn't mean anything by it! She doesn't know any better!

The pounding fury continued, and Alice thought her arms and legs would crumble into pieces. It was the strangest thing, to feel a shaking from the inside out.

Stop it! Stop it this instant! She has the Blessing of the House, and if you don't stop, I'm going to tell on you!

The hailstorm ended. Alice took a deep breath. Ivy rushed to explain.

He doesn't like the word "ghosts." He thinks it's demeaning. He prefers "spirits." It shows respect. He thinks. Ivy prattled on. *I don't care. And there are so many different kinds of us—the Settled Ones, the Past Due, the Forever Forgotten—what does it really matter if you call us "ghosts" or "spirits." The important thing is—*

We fought and won at the Battle of Saratoga. We lost with honor at the Battle of Brandywine— The stony rumbling in Alice's bones this time was more gentle. Alice looked at the shattered patch of light and saw that more and more pieces were falling to the floor, splintering into ever smaller shards.

Oh! said Ivy impatiently. *Here we go again! You've disjointed him. It's not your fault, but please don't do it again! We won't get any sense out of him until he rests in the walls.*

Troublesome whelp! grumbled Mugwort. *We fought and won at the Battle of Saratoga. We lost with honor at the Battle of Brandywine—*

It's one of the few things he remembers. We all forget—as we become forgotten. Ivy's voice grew gentle and coaxing, and Alice could tell she was speaking to Mugwort. *Yes, you did, Mugwort. With great honor . . .*

Alice felt the hairs on her head prickle as if the air were

suddenly electrified. She thought she felt a slight tremor beneath her feet.

Uh-oh, said Ivy. *We better skedaddle.*

Suddenly a shriek was heard upstairs. Alice turned to look up the curved staircase that led to the second floor. Another shriek split the air, and then silence. When she looked at the space beneath the archway, both patches of light had disappeared. Alice was alone. She felt it in every part of her body.

The next day, Alice returned to the House. There were so many questions bouncing in her brain. She hoped she would have another ghostly encounter and be able to ask a few of them, but if that was not to be, then she had brought her tools and materials to work on the fireplace. Alice didn't like to waste time.

As soon as she arrived, she emptied her canvas tool bag, which she had filled that morning with everything she could possibly need. She saw that a chunk of plaster had fallen to the floor from the ceiling. This caused her to notice the many holes and chips in the walls of the parlor. *What a mess!* she thought. Suddenly, the minor gouges in the mantelpiece didn't seem like the most urgent task at hand.

She spent the rest of the morning humming to herself as she spackled the walls, the questions in her head floating and rearranging themselves as her putty knife scraped and filled.

"Did you forget about us? Already?" asked a sharp voice that sounded like it belonged to a very impatient little girl.

Startled, Alice dropped her putty knife, splattering the bridge of her nose with spackle as the knife fell. To her complete surprise, she saw the outline of a small girl, drawn as if by a trail of smoke. The outline wavered and grew thin, then strengthened and thickened, then dissipated once more. It was as if the shape of the girl might be puffed away by the slightest breath. And yet it held itself together, fading and reforming, much like the patches of light had the day before.

"Is that you? Ivy? I can see you!" said Alice, both shocked and delighted.

"I know!" said Ivy. "You saw me *yesterday!*"

"No!" said Alice. "Yesterday I saw shimmery light, and I heard bells when you talked. Today I *see* you. And I'm *hearing* you with my ears!"

"You can actually see me?" asked Ivy excitedly. "What do I look like? What? What?" The wispy outline of the girl jumped impatiently from one foot to the other, all while hovering several feet above the floor.

"You're small," said Alice. "And delicate, although maybe that's just because you're made out of smoke. You're wearing a dress with a big bow at the neck and a little hat. You have gloves on. Your hair is very fancy, curled all around your face. And you're carrying the smallest suitcase I've ever seen."

"It's called a *valise*," she said proudly. "And that was my best dress, the one with the giant bow. I remember. I was six, and it was a big day. We were going on a trip! And I insisted on packing and carrying my *own* suitcase." Ivy held the small case up to show Alice. "I threw a *fit*! So my mother gave me this little valise, and she said I could put anything in it that I wanted. I don't even remember what I packed, but they were all my most special things. I was so excited. I was going on a trip!"

"Where were you going?" asked Alice.

Ivy shook her head. "I don't remember. But I was so eager. Impatient! My parents were taking forever. The cab was waiting out front. I went outside. I wanted to go! But my parents weren't ready." The features on her face shifted as she tried to remember the details.

"Ivy, are you sure you were six? You talk like you were older than that."

"Well, I *am* very old. I'm one of the Past Due, and we do pick up new things in the changing world, even if we're no longer a part of it. We watch. We learn."

"I thought you were a ghost."

"Ghost, yes, but then there are all different kinds," explained Ivy. "A Past Due or a Settled One. A Wanderer. A Captive. Some of us are . . ." Ivy's voice trailed off. She looked down at the small suitcase in her hand. "Let's not talk about that. I'm going on a trip today! I'm very excited!"

"Ivy," said Alice gently. "I think that was a long time ago. You're not going on a trip anymore."

"Oh. I think you're right. Time is so hard to keep hold of when you're a Past Due," said Ivy.

"What *is* that?" asked Alice. "What's a Past Due?"

"*Um*. 'Expired,' I would say. Like a bill that hasn't been

paid. Or a library book that needs to be returned. It means we've died, but we can't move on to become a Settled One. Someday, though. I hope."

"Why can't you move on?" asked Alice. It was getting harder and harder to make out Ivy's wispy outline. Her edges were growing faint.

"Unfinished Business of the Heart! Not *my* fault! At least I don't think so . . . I was only six . . ."

Suddenly Ivy raised her head, and her outline became as sharp as the edge of a razor. "I have to go now," she said urgently. "The House . . ."

She vanished, and Alice just barely caught her final words: "*. . . is displeased.*"

Chapter 6

It wasn't until she was packing up her canvas bag in the afternoon that Alice became aware someone was watching her. The shadows across the parlor floor were long, and the sun was low in the sky. It was later than she had meant to stay. She sensed the eyes on her and turned, surprised to see another smoke-outlined figure, but one as different from Ivy as possible. This person was a soldier, nearly six feet tall, with a curled wig and a tricorn hat on his head. He had smoky epaulets on his shoulders and rows of buttons along each side of his coat that disappeared and then re-formed.

"Mugwort?" asked Alice.

The vaporous soldier bowed stiffly, seeming almost to

break in half at the waist before his misty outline reasserted itself. Alice noticed he was carrying a sword strapped to his side as if he had just come from battle.

"Is that what you were wearing when you died?" asked Alice, not sure if this was an indelicate question. She was new to ghost etiquette and bound to make some mistakes.

"This is my burial costume," he said formally, his voice still rough and gravelly. "I lived in this house for many years. It was my final home, my final resting place. I died in my bed, in my nightshirt."

"You look very nice," said Alice.

Mugwort growled. "I was a soldier. Soldiers do not 'look nice.' We look honorable. We look ready. We look brave. Not nice. When you have fought with men such as I have, you learn to look beneath the surface of appearances and value what matters most: integrity."

"Do you remember much . . . from your life?" Again, Alice worried that she was being rude without meaning to.

"I was a highly decorated captain. There were ten in my company, all local men, homegrown and proud to defend their farms and their families. I was respected, in this community and on the battlefield. There's a book about me at the college library. Betimes, I sit beside it."

"You go to the college library?" Alice wondered if Mugwort had ever been there when she had been there. The thought sent a slight shiver up her spine.

"Betimes," answered Mugwort.

"Do you meet other spirits when you're out . . . wandering?"

"Our paths may cross, but to little purpose. A gentleman of my rank and position doesn't mingle with every Past Due he meets."

"But aren't you—?" Alice stopped herself midsentence. Perhaps asking Mugwort if he were a Past Due himself was impertinent. She didn't want to offend. So instead, she asked one of the questions that had been floating and rearranging themselves in her head since her morning conversation with Ivy. "What is a Captive?"

Mugwort stiffened, and the shifting outline of his face became rigid. "It goes without saying that a Captive is one who cannot Wander, one who is locked forever inside the house in which it passed. I don't associate with Captives. They have committed grievous crimes and don't deserve our mercy." Mugwort began to march toward the wall as if he would march straight through it.

"Wait," pleaded Alice, realizing she had aggravated him and hoping to soothe him so that he would stay longer. "Tell me more about the book. Why do you sit beside it? Don't you read it?"

"Foolish child! Spirits are not able to hold things or turn pages in the physical world." He paused and looked out the window at the towering sycamore tree. "I planted that tree," he said, before adding bitterly, "It will outlast me." He turned to look at Alice. "I sit beside the book because it replenishes my heart to see it. The book is the last evidence that I lived, and so long as the book remains, I remain."

Alice opened her mouth to ask another question but feared that she would send Mugwort fleeing into the walls. He stared morosely out the window.

"I fought alongside Washington. He died but two weeks before I did. People remember him today. I hear them speak of him. They will always remember General George Washington."

"I'm sure people remember you, too," said Alice hoping to cheer him up. "You fought and won at the Battle of Saratoga. You lost with honor at the Battle of Brandywine." Cautiously, she added, "What was your name when you were alive?"

"I don't remember. Names are easily shed, easily forgotten, easily erased. They are the least important thing we carry from cradle to coffin."

"I bet I could do an internet search and find you in about five minutes," said Alice.

Mugwort scowled. "I have heard of this interestnet. There, all manner of murk and muddiness resides. Do not presume to tell me what I already know. Good afternoon to you, miss!" He performed a curt bow in her direction and began to fade. Alice still had so many questions she wanted to ask.

"Wait! So, just to be clear, you *are* one of the Past Due? Like Ivy?" she blurted out.

A draft blew in from the foyer, and Mugwort's smoky outline disappeared. His final words lingered in the air: "I am."

Alice stood still, staring at the spot where Mugwort had

been, then exhaled loudly. "What is it with these ghosts?" she said in exasperation.

Instantly, Mugwort reappeared, his outline sharper than before. "Do *not* call me that word. I am a *spirit!*"

"Yes! Of course you are. My apologies! I'll remember, I promise." Alice barreled ahead with her question. "So, you have Unfinished Business of the Heart?"

"I do." Mugwort stood stiffly, as if overseeing a military drill.

"What does that mean?" asked Alice.

"It means exactly what it says."

"I don't understand."

"You are addled," said Mugwort. But he grabbed ahold of both lapels of his jacket, and Alice recognized the look of one who is about to begin a lecture.

"There are four categories of Unfinished Business of the Heart. The first is neglecting to tell someone you love them before you die. The second is betraying someone you love without making amends before you die. The third is departing this earth angry at someone you love, such that said person must live for the rest of his life with your anger, unresolved. The fourth is, well, I would suggest you ask Ivy about *that* one."

"But which one is yours?" asked Alice.

"I do not remember what my Unfinished Business of the Heart is." Mugwort drifted to the window. Alice was not surprised to see that his vaporous figure cast no shadow at all.

"We often forget. Sometimes it is better, but in this case, I am doomed by it. If I cannot remember my Unfinished Business, then I cannot finish it, and when my time runs out, I will become a Forever Forgotten." He bowed his head. "It is a dishonor." Once again, his wispy outline began to blow apart, dissolving right before Alice's eyes.

"Wait," shouted Alice. "What do you mean, when your time runs out?"

Mugwort's voice floated out of the walls: "The book remains."

He was gone.

Alice was left alone standing in the now dark parlor. How had it gotten so late? The Rule of Potchnik! *Estimate that talking to any ghost will take three times as long as you expect!*

Alice finished packing up. As she put the last of her tools in the canvas bag, she heard footsteps coming up the stone walkway. Her heart began to beat faster. The footsteps stopped outside the front door. She held her breath. Who could it be? Why would anyone be prowling around a condemned house?

Alice heard a knock at the door. The front door was unlocked! She had left it open since the first day she had visited the House in case she needed a quick exit. Now she wanted to kick herself for being so careless. She had been certain the CONDEMNED sign would keep away any intruders.

Was it the police? she wondered. Or the fire department?

"Hello?" said a voice on the other side of the door.

Alice knew that voice! It was her father! But why in the

world would he come to this old, condemned house?

"Hello?" he called again.

Alice's heart called out to him, *I'm here, Dad!* But her mouth remained silent. She wasn't ready to share the mystery of the House or its inhabitants. Not even with her father and mother. She needed time to understand what this all meant: Ivy and Mugwort and the beating heart of the House. She wanted to learn everything she could, and she wanted to do it alone.

She heard her father's hand on the doorknob. She saw the knob begin to turn. She put her hand over her mouth and willed her heart to stop beating. There must be no noise to give her away. He must not find her here.

The doorknob stopped. Her father's hand on the other side rattled it and then gave up.

The door was locked. But by whom?

Alice heard her father tap softly on the cardboard sign taped to the front door. She knew he was not a man who broke rules. In fact, his life's work was devoted to following the rules and making sure that others did too. No one was supposed to enter a condemned house. He knew the dangers. Again, Alice wondered why he was there.

She heard him sigh, then start to walk back down the pathway to the sidewalk. Alice felt her body relax. She hadn't even realized how tightly she'd been gripping her toes until she let them go. But how had the door become locked? Alice was *positive* she had left it open from the very first day. Was it the

House keeping her father out? And if so, why?

Before she could sort any of it out, Alice heard the retreating footsteps of her father pause, and then he called out softly, "Alice?"

There was a moment of agonizing silence, and then again, "Alice?'

In that instant, Alice realized why he had come in the dark to explore the abandoned house next door. He was worried. Terribly, terribly worried about her. And suddenly she realized just how late it was and how dark it had become, and she should have been home an hour ago, but she had gotten so caught up in talking with Ivy and Mugwort that she had forgotten her parents completely.

Daddy! she wanted to call out, to set his heart at rest, to let him know that she was safe and that he had found her.

"Let him go," said Mugwort's gravelly voice from within the walls.

And then Ivy chimed in, "Let him go."

And she did. The sound of the footsteps died away in the darkness.

"Now slip out the back," instructed Ivy, "and then wait five minutes outside. When you get home, you'll seem very cold, as if you just walked a long way. They'll scold you, but they'll forgive you, because they'll be so relieved that you've come home. Now go."

As Alice hurried down the hallway to the back door, she heard their voices.

"I suppose that's what it's like *not* to be forgotten," Mugwort said bitterly.

Ivy didn't answer. The last thing Alice heard before slipping out the door was the lonely ring of a single bell. If Alice had been asked, she would have said it was the sound of crying.

"I just don't understand all the mystery about where you've been," said Alice's mother. She was making hot chocolate for Alice, feeling terrible because she had hugged her daughter so hard the minute Alice walked in the door that she had accidentally tweaked a muscle in Alice's neck.

Alice had managed to explain her lateness without actually lying, but only because her parents were not the type to interrogate. They trusted Alice. Knowing this broke Alice's heart a little bit, but not enough to tell them about the House. If she had, she knew that her mother would apply for a grant to research the House, and Alice's father would no doubt be desperate to join in the renovations. For now, Alice needed this project to be her own.

"We don't want you out after dark, pomegranate," said Alice's father, crossing his arms over his barrel-shaped chest. He stood in the middle of the kitchen, with its cracked countertops and buckled floorboards. Alice's mother stopped stirring the cocoa and stood right beside him. She, too, crossed both arms.

This maneuver was known as the Double Cross in the Cannoli-Potchnik household, and it meant that both parents were in complete agreement and there would be no more discussion. The first time the Double Cross had been employed was when Alice was just two years old and her parents had told her, "You may *not* put the cat's tail in your mouth." Since then, the Double Cross hadn't been used more than a dozen times, as Alice's mother and father often held very different points of view on child-rearing. After all, she was a Cannoli and he was a Potchnik. Luckily for them, they enjoyed a spirited disagreement and always found a way to compromise that left everyone feeling jolly and very much loved.

When Alice saw the Double Cross, she immediately promised always to be home before dark. In exchange, she asked her parents to stop asking questions about her current study project until she was ready to tell them. They agreed, and the entire family sat down to a meal of leftover pizza and chocolate rugelach, because amidst all the worry about Alice, no one had thought to cook dinner.

After her parents left for work the next morning, Alice bicycled to the college library. As she crossed the college green, she passed Carrie Tower, which was the most prominent edifice on campus. Every brochure cover for the college featured the bell tower, made of red brick and adorned with elaborate stonework. Alice supposed it was because the tower stood ninety-five feet tall and therefore gave the impression that the college was to be taken seriously.

The college library, on the other hand, failed to impress

in every way. The windows either didn't open or wouldn't close, the photocopier was perpetually broken, and the security gate, which was supposed to set off an alarm whenever an unchecked book left the premises, hadn't worked in years. It could not be denied: The library was small and shabby. Then again, the college was small and shabby too, and the library suited it well. It had the benefit of being unpretentious and full of strange things tucked in odd corners. Alice loved it.

She was greeted by Mrs. Fein, her favorite librarian, who cheerfully reminded Alice that one of the books Alice had checked out—the enormous one on architecture—was overdue. "Be sure to bring it back next time or renew it online," said Mrs. Fein. Alice remembered that the book was still tucked under the brick steps of the porch of her house, and she promised Mrs. Fein she would bring it back soon.

Mrs. Fein looked very much like a beetle. She dressed from head to toe in black and scurried about with alarming speed, as if she had more than two legs to get her where she needed to go. She wore her jet-black, shoulder-length hair slicked back into a hard shell using a great deal of product. And even indoors, she wore large reflective prescription sunglasses, which she claimed protected her eyes from an extreme light sensitivity. Alice often wondered if Mrs. Fein had secret antennae that could pop up when she needed them, because she always knew what was going on, even in the farthest reaches of the dusty old library.

"Thanks, Mrs. Fein. Does the library have any history

books on famous people who lived in this town?"

Mrs. Fein tapped her black-polished fingernails together as she always did when thinking. "I don't believe any famous people *have* lived in this town," she said, "but I'll check." Her fingers clicked furiously on the keys of her computer. *"Hmm!* Actually, there's one book. But it was written in 1915. Let me show you where it is." She scurried to the Local History 371.01 section of the library and pulled a slim book bound in green leather from the shelf. As she looked at it in her hand, she smiled as if at a joke.

"What's funny?" asked Alice.

"This short book has the longest title I've ever seen. *Millbrook, with Interest: Which being a modest collection of glimpses wherein may be seen how those who came before us worked and played, sinned and worshipped, hoped and feared, and otherwise comported themselves much as we ourselves still do today in the town of Millbrook."*

"I can't believe they can fit all that on one page," said Alice.

"Small type," said Mrs. Fein, handing the book to her.

It didn't take Alice long to find the chapter on Mugwort, whose living name was Nathaniel Finch. He'd been a decorated captain in the Revolutionary War and a successful manufacturer of gunpowder before and during the war. In fact, he'd made a fortune selling gunpowder. And when the war was over, he'd built the finest house in three counties. There was even a photograph of it in the book: the House as it had looked in 1915. Nathaniel Finch had died after catching pneumonia on a late-season hunting trip. The brief history made no mention of any Unfinished Business of the Heart.

Well, at least I know his name, thought Alice. *It's a start.*

When Alice returned the book to Mrs. Fein, she asked her, "When was the last time this book was checked out?" She thought it might cheer up the gloomy Mugwort to know that people were still reading about his life.

Mrs. Fein tapped away at the keys of the computer, then scrolled down the page, letting out a whirring exhale. "Wow. According to the computer, never. This book hasn't circulated since we began recording data, which was more than fifty years ago."

Alice frowned. This was not good news. Maybe Mugwort was right. He'd been forgotten.

"Thank you for pointing this out, Alice," said Mrs. Fein, scooping up the book and placing it on a shelf behind the desk alongside some other tattered volumes. "I'm always looking for books to cull from the collection." She picked up one of the other books to be discarded. "Mouse damage. We have a terrible problem here in the library."

"You're taking those books out of circulation?" Alice felt herself growing panicked at the thought. This could not be good.

"Don't worry. We recycle."

Recycle? The only book that recorded Mugwort's life? Alice needed to think of something, and quick.

"Well, if you don't want that book, can *I* have it?" asked

Alice, her palms sweating.

"I'm sorry, Alice," said Mrs. Fein, shaking her head sympathetically but firmly. "There's a whole review process for removing books from the collection. And then we sell them in the annual Friends sale. I can't just give them away."

Alice wished more than anything that she hadn't asked Mrs. Fein about the book's circulation record. What a terrible mistake she had made.

As she bicycled home, the bell in Carrie Tower tolled the hour in a way that was both ominous and sad. Alice tried to figure out how to tell Mugwort the two pieces of news she had: that she had discovered his living name and that she had helped destroy the last piece of evidence that he had ever existed.

Alice had been sanding the walls for only a few minutes when Ivy appeared. Was it Alice's imagination, or did Ivy seem a little more . . . there? A little more substantial. Less wispy. Alice thought she could see details on Ivy's dress and the valise that hadn't been visible the day before. And though the edges of Ivy still wobbled, they seemed more steady.

"Ivy!" said Alice. "I'm glad you're here, I—" Alice stopped abruptly and looked at Ivy. "Have you been crying?"

"Ghosts don't cry," said Ivy heavily. "We're too drippy. But someone died."

"Oh, Ivy! I'm so sorry." Alice reached out to put a hand on her friend's shoulder, but her hand just passed through the cool vapor that was Ivy. "Were you very close?"

"I didn't know her at all."

Alice was surprised. "Then why are you sad?"

"It means I have less time."

Alice remembered that Mugwort had said the same thing: he was running out of time. "What does that mean?" she asked. "I thought once you were a ghost, time didn't matter."

"Oh, it matters, at least if you're a Past Due. The Past Due need to finish their business so that they can become one of the Settled Ones. But we don't have forever. When the last person who remembers your name dies, or the last photograph is lost, or the last newspaper article is destroyed, your time is up! You become a Forever Forgotten, and they say it's a terrible fate."

Alice was beginning to understand the seriousness of Unfinished Business. "Who died?"

"My sister. She was born after I died, so she never knew me, but my parents told her stories about me. And now she's gone. And she was probably one of the last people on earth who remembered me. I'm not lucky like Mugwort. I don't have a book written about me. Who would write a book about a six-year-old?"

Alice bit her lip, a bad Cannoli habit. She was still trying to figure out a way to rescue Mugwort's book. "He's not *so* lucky. He can't even remember what his Unfinished Business is. Do you remember yours?"

"Of course I do," said Ivy impatiently.

A gust of air blew down the chimney, spewing a plume of soot and ashes into the room.

"Well. Someone isn't happy," said Ivy. "I guess I've said too much."

"What do you mean?" whispered Alice.

"There's no point in whispering," said Ivy. "A whisper is as good as a shout. The House knows *everything* that goes on within its walls. Remember that. You can't hide anything. Don't even try."

The curtain rods over both parlor windows crashed to the floor.

"I'm going! I'm going!" said Ivy. "You're the one who gave her the Blessing of the House!" And Ivy flew straight up and disappeared through the ceiling.

Chapter 7

No ghosts visited Alice the next day as she worked on repairing the walls of the parlor, and yet she could tell she was being watched. Carefully. Sometimes the hair on her arm stood up for no reason; sometimes she felt a breeze blow through the room when the air outside was still; sometimes she almost thought she could hear a whispered voice. By the end of the day, the walls were prepped.

The next morning she began to paint, spreading the creamy yellow color like butter on toast. A breath of air flowed from the second floor, sweeping down the long staircase and swirling through the foyer. To Alice, it sounded like a deep sigh of contentment.

Once or twice, she thought she heard a noise overhead. A bang or a thud. The muffled sound of breaking glass.

But no one appeared, and when Alice asked questions into the air, she received no answers. Quiet usually comforted Alice, but this particular silence felt like abandonment.

Being a Potchnik, she continued to work. She finished painting the walls, repaired the brackets for the fallen curtain rods, dry-cleaned the drapes and rehung them, and repaired the frames for two old oil paintings that she then hung on the walls. One was of a ship safe in its harbor, and one was of a ship tossed in a storm at sea. Together, they gave the room a lively feeling, a feeling that this was a house where people lived and loved and danced and died. More than a house; a home.

On the fourth day, Alice examined the moldering sofa. It had clearly served as a nest for many families of mice over the years. Though the mice were gone, they had chewed through the cushions in at least a dozen places. The sofa would need a complete redo.

Alice had no skill in upholstery, but she knew someone who did: Roberta, who was the head of the costume shop in the Theater Arts Department. Roberta had a way of coaxing an ordinary scrap of fabric to be its best self, and she scavenged odd remnants from flea markets and secondhand shops, hoarding stray bolts of cloth as if they were gold.

The question was how to get the sofa to the Theater Arts building, which was all the way on the other side of campus.

Luckily, Dave had some free time in the morning. Alice was able to drag the sofa out of the House and onto the weedy lawn of the Cannoli-Potchnik house before Dave arrived, and it didn't occur to him to ask why she had carried it out herself instead of waiting for him. He simply hefted it into his truck and drove away.

It had been five days since Alice had seen Ivy, and she began to wonder if the House had taken its blessing away. Or perhaps Ivy and Mugwort were tired of her and had forgotten about her in the way that ghosts do. Alice was surprised how much these thoughts hurt, as if someone had punched her in the stomach, leaving her with an ache that wouldn't go away. She was glad there was a repair task—and a difficult one—ahead of her. It would help distract her from this empty feeling.

It was time to begin work on the scarred and rotten floor in the parlor. She'd already found some salvaged boards that were a good match and could be used to replace the worst of the rot. It would take weeks to refinish the old floor, but now that the sofa was gone, the work could begin.

On the day that Alice began to rip up the floor, she lifted her eyes from the nail she'd been prying and saw Ivy seated in midair by the fireplace. Her valise rested on her small lap.

"I didn't forget you," said Ivy in her six-year-old voice, which gave Alice the uncomfortable feeling that Ivy *could* read her mind. Then again, maybe it was just the kind of thing anyone would say after a long absence.

"Well, you didn't stay," said Alice, returning to her work. She had a glimpse into her mother's meaning from that last lecture: that staying was important and leaving left a mark. Alice really had been very hurt by Ivy's abandonment, even more than she had realized until this moment.

"I'm sorry," said Ivy. "There was nothing I could do. There are rules, and the House sets them."

"Why would the House make a rule like that? Not letting you visit me? That seems mean." Alice yanked on the nail with such force that it came out of the wood with a shriek and went flying across the room. She fell back, then shouted up the staircase, "Are you mean?"

Ivy circled the room quickly, then settled restlessly near the chandelier, as if preparing for a quick exit though the ceiling. "I told you before, you don't need to shout to be heard. The House . . ." She paused. "The House has a great strength and knowledge that it draws from the stone of the earth, which is older than time itself. It understands things we never can. The House *always* knows what's best."

Alice thought about her days of loneliness and the sting of feeling forgotten. What purpose had been served by that?

"The House," continued Ivy, "is where I was born and where I died. It's the only home I've ever known. That's a powerful thing, right there. The power of *home*. I couldn't go against it. But I'm sorry I hurt you."

Alice wasn't one to hold on to anger or reject a heartfelt apology. Especially from Ivy.

"Okay," said Alice, getting back to her feet. "But I still have questions." She raised her voice to a moderate shout. "And I'm going to ask them!"

"Criminy!" said Ivy, looking nervously up the staircase. "Don't make so much noise!"

"Here's what I want to know," said Alice, bending down to work on another stubborn nail. "Mugwort said there were four categories of Unfinished Business of the Heart, and he told me the first three: not telling a person you love them, betraying someone you love, and dying when you're angry at a person you love. So, what's the fourth?"

The features on Ivy's face blew away like sand in a windstorm, then reappeared in resolute formation. "The worst of all: I died with an overdue library book."

Alice laughed. "I'm serious! I want to know what your Unfinished Business is. I want to help. I want to help both of you become Settled Ones."

"That *is* my Unfinished Business." Ivy stamped her ghostly foot in midair. "The fourth way is to die when you have an overdue library book. Until the book is returned, you remain one of the Past Due. That's where it gets its name."

"A *library book*?" asked Alice. "That's ridiculous!"

"It is *not*," said Ivy, truly offended. "Libraries are sacred places. Think about it. A library gives everything and asks nothing in return. It gives to the rich and to the poor, to the young and to the old, to the healthy and the sick. Tell me another place on earth that does that? It is *grievous* Unfinished

Business to fail to return a library book—a treasure that is given with the solemn promise to bring it back. There's no betrayal greater than that!"

"I suppose," said Alice dubiously. "So, where's the book? The one you didn't return when you died?"

"I have no idea," said Ivy. "I know I put it somewhere safe. It was brand-new, and I was the very first person to check it out. I hid it because I loved it so much. And now look where it's gotten me!"

"What was the title?"

Ivy twirled as a way to show she had no answer.

"Do you remember what it was about?" asked Alice.

Ivy clutched her valise and concentrated. "There was a rabbit. And he had wonderful pajamas with blue stripes." Then she shrugged. "When you're only six years old, you don't think about consequences. Like waiting for your parents when you're going on a trip. And staying out of the road, even though you're so excited and the cab is right there, waiting."

Alice knew there was a time to ask questions and a time to keep quiet. This was a time to keep quiet. She could feel the House all around them. There was a sense of anticipation, as if the House were at the ready, prepared to protect Ivy if she ventured too far into this particular memory.

Ivy shrugged again, a wistful smile on her face. "A simple library book. Who knew?"

"We'll find it, Ivy," said Alice.

Ivy looked closely at her. "Do you really want to help us?" she asked. "*All* of us?"

"Yes!" said Alice quickly, then stopped short. "Wait. What do you mean, 'all of us'?"

"You haven't met Danny yet," said Ivy. "Well, the House named him Dandelion, but it would be cruel to call him that. And honestly, if there's just one of us you can help, it should be him, because he's driving us crazy."

"There's another ghost? A Past Due? Why haven't I seen him?"

"He never comes out. Never. He hasn't left the walls for more than fifty years. At this point, he's simply *seeped into* the plaster, his essence spread like a mold in the gap between the wood. His form is completely disorganized. He's moody and melancholy. Unable to do anything except *wail*! Night and day!" Ivy pressed her hand to her forehead as if she had a terrible headache. "You can imagine what that's like!"

Alice couldn't imagine it at all, but it sounded horrible.

"I'm telling you, if we don't get him out of the walls and on his way to being a Settled One, Mugwort and I might petition the House for removal to another dwelling. We just can't take it anymore. The noise! And the negative energy! Some days he drains us to the point where *we* can't get out." Ivy picked up her valise and started to drift toward the wall.

"Is that who makes the noise?" asked Alice. "The crashing overhead. And the shrieking?"

Ivy hovered, as if she couldn't make up her mind to go

forward or back. "Yes," she said slowly. "It's Danny who makes those noises." Ivy began to drift toward the wall again.

"Wait!" Alice stopped her. "Is that *all* of you? You, Mugwort, and Danny?" Alice wanted to help, but it was already feeling like a much bigger project than she had estimated. *The Rule of Potchnik!* "I need to know, Ivy," said Alice. "One, two, three. No more ghosts after that?"

"No," said Ivy, not looking at Alice as she spoke. "No one like us. Bluebird's honor." Alice thought she saw Ivy's eyes flicker for an instant toward the grand staircase just before her wispy outline disappeared like a candle being snuffed out, leaving behind a single trail of smoke.

The mid-September light was fading. Alice slipped out the back door and walked to her own house under threatening clouds. Her hand was on the latch of the front door when she heard the first crack of thunder.

Chapter 8

The Cannoli-Potchnik house leaked. Everywhere.

In fact, it seemed to Alice as though there were more holes than roof over their heads.

They had used every container in the house to catch the dripping water: salad bowls, teacups, Tupperware, vases, spaghetti pots, drinking glasses, pie plates, and even the teakettle. Alice, her mother, and her father took turns patrolling the containers to make sure they didn't overflow onto the warped and rotted floors.

The good news was that the largest leak in the bathroom ceiling was right over the toilet, so they didn't need to find another container to catch the dripping water. The bad news was that when they needed to "use the facilities," they had to hold an umbrella over their heads. It was a tricky bit of balancing, but with the combined family traits of Cannoli flexibility and Potchnik strength, they managed. Alice's family was exceptionally adaptable, and the three of them made the best of the situation with gusto and good cheer.

Alice was thinking about the architecture book, still safely stowed under the front porch. She knew the book was protected from the rain, but she wondered if the overwhelming dampness of the air would cause damage. Then again, bringing the book inside the house would do little good—it was raining nearly as hard inside as out. Alice decided to leave the book where it was. It would be fine.

She walked into the dining room where her mother was grading papers. "Mom?" said Alice. "Do we have an International House?"

Professor Cannoli's red pen moved swiftly across the paper she was reading. Without looking up, she said, "I need more context."

"Wait . . . is that comment for me?" asked Alice. "Or are you writing it on the paper you're grading?"

"Both," said Professor Cannoli, finishing her writing with a flourish. "Thomas Schlumberg . . . never provides context! But in this case, I was successfully multitasking. What do you mean?"

"Does the college have an International House building?" asked Alice. "Where international students live?"

Professor Cannoli snorted. "We don't attract international students. Which is a pity! They'd add some vibrancy to the campus, and I'm told they pay *full* tuition!"

"Did we *ever* have an International House?"

"Not to my knowledge. But check with Professor Erasmus. She speaks twelve languages, and she's ninety-three years old. If we ever did have international students, she would have been the one talking to them."

"Alice!" said Professor Erasmus with glee. "I haven't seen you since the fall of the Roman Empire!"

"Hi, Professor Erasmus," said Alice, smiling at the tiny, birdlike woman sitting behind her massive desk holding a cup of coffee. Professor Erasmus was so old that her spine was shaped like a C, which meant she spent most of her time staring down at her own feet, often sporting high-top sneakers covered in sequins. She liked the ankle support *and* the glam. She had a twinkly spirit, too, and Alice loved visiting her office, which was filled with treasures collected from years of travel all over the world.

Professor Erasmus held a hot cup of coffee under her nose and sniffed deeply. The steam swirled around her head. "I'm not allowed to drink it. Diverticulitis! But I sniff a cup every morning and another one at four in the afternoon. I swear it gives me an energy boost!" Her eyes sparkled with delight. "What brings you to the world of foreign languages?"

"I have a question," said Alice. "Were there ever international students here at the college?"

"Wouldn't that have been splendid! All those languages! But no," sighed Professor Erasmus. "Never. Not even one. The college tried in the late sixties. It even bought an old house on the edge of campus and named it the International House to attract them. Like bees to the honey, the dean of faculty said. The idea was *If you build it, they will come!* They did not!"

"Why?"

"We're too small. We're too . . . ordinary."

Ordinary! thought Alice. *If only you knew!* "Did anything interesting ever happen at that . . . International House?"

Professor Erasmus sniffed deeply and shook her head. Coils of steam poured out of her cup, entwining themselves in the old woman's hair. "As far as I know, nothing. It was just a regular dorm, like all the others. They closed the building after only a few years. Too expensive to heat. Even the dean admitted the plan had been a failure. The last year the International House was used by the college was 1972. I'm sure if you look in the reference section of the library archives—"

Professor Erasmus suddenly stopped sniffing. She put her coffee mug down. "There *was* something. I'd forgotten. 1972. The year the International House closed. A boy died. I don't remember his name."

Alice's heart began to beat faster. "How did he die?"

By now, Professor Erasmus's entire head was surrounded by the fog from the steaming cup of coffee. It swirled and tendrilled about her face and hair, like growing vines, and Alice almost thought she could see the vanishings and reappearance of a face. "Well, it's just too silly," said Professor Erasmus. "But the rumor on campus was that he died of a *broken heart*!"

"Is that even possible?" asked Alice.

Professor Erasmus tapped her beaklike nose. "I'm an old woman, but there are still some things *I* can't explain. As someone we both know once said, 'There are more things in heaven and Earth, Horatio, than are dreamt of in your philosophy.'"

"Shakespeare," said Alice. She stared at the final trail of steam as it corkscrewed its way up to the ceiling and disappeared.

"Well cited! You are your mother's daughter!" Professor Erasmus smiled with delight, then looked with great displeasure into her coffee cup. She dipped an arthritic finger into the black liquid. "My coffee's gone stone cold! Just like that!" She put the mug down with a grumble of dissatisfaction.

"Can't you still sniff it?" asked Alice.

"Not the same. Different smell."

"Oh." Alice knew something that could make coffee go stone cold in an instant, but it seemed to have left the room through the ceiling. "Professor Erasmus?" asked Alice. "What does the word 'dereliction' mean? I mean, I know what it *means*, mostly. But where does the word come from?"

Professor Erasmus's disgruntled face lit up. She loved etymology even more than she loved coffee. "*Dereliction!* Such a rich word! It has many meanings, depending on the context."

There was that word again, thought Alice: *context*. Her mother often said, "Context is everything."

Professor Erasmus continued, enraptured. "The word comes from the Latin verb *derelinquere*, which means 'to neglect' or more directly from the Latin noun *derelictio*, which means, roughly, 'an abandonment.' So, as a noun, it means the state of having been abandoned and become dilapidated. Or having fallen into ruin. But it has a second meaning, which is 'the shameful failure to fulfill one's obligations.'"

Alice thought carefully. "You mean, leaving one's business unfinished? If you have an obligation—in business—and you don't do it, then it's a shameful thing."

Professor Erasmus nodded. "Yes, you're considered 'derelict in your duties.' And yes, it is rather shameful. It's important to take care of one's obligations, don't you think, Alice?"

"Ye-e-e-s," said Alice slowly, thinking of her own promise to settle three ghosts. "But sometimes things happen. And you don't have time. Or things are harder than you expected. It seems kind of mean to make someone feel ashamed about that."

"That's why I say, 'Never put off until tomorrow what you can do today.'"

Alice looked at Professor Erasmus and knew that she would be one of the happy Settled Ones. Still wearing her sequined high-tops, no doubt.

"Ivy!" shouted Alice, leaving her bicycle on her own front lawn and bursting into the House. "You were *there*!"

A tiny puff of vapor rose up from the parlor floor, but it refused to take shape. The wisps coalesced in a shifting cloud of murkiness, then wafted and dissipated. "Form yourself this minute!" said Alice sternly. "And call the boy!"

The vapor settled by the fireplace, and Alice could see that it didn't move as Ivy's essence did. There were no long tendrils reaching like vines. Instead, this fog was heavy and dissolute, dissolving over and over again before it could form itself into anything definite. It seemed to Alice that there was rain falling within the small ecosystem of the collected vapor.

"Danny?" asked Alice tentatively. "We haven't met. I'm Alice."

"I know," came a voice so low that Alice took a step forward, afraid she would miss what was said next. But nothing more was said.

Alice shifted from one foot to the other, completely at a loss for how to proceed. Luckily, she remembered her mother's sound advice: *You'll never learn anything interesting if you don't ask questions!*

"Did someone break your heart?" asked Alice gently.

A wailing sound, like a cross between a screaming baby and a fire-engine siren, poured forth from the murkiness. It was a noise so swollen with pain that Alice had to cover both ears to keep herself from running out of the room.

"You see!" said Ivy, filtering through the wall and swirling around the room in an agitated manner. "It is un*bearable*!"

Alice remembered another piece of advice from her resolute

mother: *Sometimes, honey pie, you just need to get a grip!*

"Danny!" said Alice. "Get a grip! GET! A! GRIP!"

The wailing stopped, as abruptly as if someone had snuffed out a candle flame.

Alice turned to Ivy. "Ivy!" she said sternly. "You were in Professor Erasmus's office this morning."

"So?" said Ivy impertinently. "I'm allowed to Wander."

"Well, you ruined her morning cup of coffee, and I don't think that's very nice."

Alice turned back to the smudgy cloud of misery that was Danny's form. "Now *listen* to me," she said. "It's okay to feel sad about things, and it's perfectly okay to cry, but that— *that!*—what you were just doing—is not allowed. It's like having a hundred pins poked into my eardrums. So if you do that again, I'm going to have to leave *immediately*! And then I won't be able to help you. Do you get it?"

Alice watched as the dense and dripping fog slowly twisted and wrenched itself into a shape: the shape of a young man, college age by the look of his raggedy T-shirt and jeans. The message on his T-shirt kept shifting from "No Nukes" to "Earth Day" to "US Out of Vietnam NOW!" His shaggy, unkempt hair fell forward over his eyes, which gazed dispiritedly at the floor, as if the weight of his cloudlike head was too much to hold up.

"Okay," said Alice, looking to Ivy for strength and confidence. "Now, *without weeping*, tell me what you remember about your Unfinished Business."

Alice listened as Danny unspooled his story. He was the newest of the three ghosts and remembered much more of his living past than Ivy or Mugwort.

When he died, he had been a senior majoring in computer science. His parents thought it was a silly thing to study and that computers were nothing more than big pinball machines. They were certain there was no future in computing. Danny was good at coding, but he loved poetry, too. It was in the class Romantic Poets of the Early Nineteenth Century where he met a young woman named Jenny Gurkenstein.

"Wait!" Alice interrupted. "You remember *her* name, but you don't remember your own?"

"*Love,*" whispered Ivy.

Danny continued. Jenny was a music major, with a wicked interest in computers and coding. She said writing music and writing code were a lot alike. Danny fell in love and wrote her sixty-three love poems, but he never showed any of them to her. "She was so smart and talented," said Danny. "I could never tell her my feelings." Alice watched as the rainstorm within Danny began to pelt his insides, pounding the fragile outline of his spirit form until it looked as though he would break into pieces. He lifted his eyes to the ceiling, and his mouth opened wide.

"STOP!" commanded Alice. "No wailing. Where are the poems?"

"I hid them," said Danny, "so that no one would ever find them."

"What is it with ghosts and hiding?" Alice asked Ivy, exasperated. "You and your library book, Danny and his poems?" She turned back to Danny. "Where did you hide them?"

"I don't remember."

Alice groaned. "Well, which room in the House was yours?" But Danny couldn't answer. He was beginning to howl again. "Go back into the walls," shouted Alice, covering both ears.

"You see what I mean?" asked Ivy, once he was gone. "You have *got* to get him Settled. Mugwort and I can't take it anymore."

Alice stared at the spot where the melancholy ghost had disappeared. As if to herself, she whispered, "Ivy, Mugwort, Dandelion." They were the invasive weeds that grew in the yard around the House.

Ivy drifted in front of Alice and then stretched out one arm. The smoky outline of her limb dissolved and transformed into words, a ribbon of letters wafting out from her shoulder: *I know which room.* The words wavered and wobbled, then disappeared as soon as Alice read them.

Alice watched as Ivy drifted into the foyer and floated to the top of the staircase. Fearfully, she reached out one vaporous arm, which stretched and lengthened until it reached a closed door on the second floor. Alice took note: It was the third one on the left.

Ivy's arm had now retracted almost to its usual form, but at the last instant it shaped itself into a single word: *DON'T.*

Alice looked at Ivy. Her outline was so thin, it looked like it was made of spiderwebs, and all her tendrils drooped like flowers in a heavy rain. Alice understood that this had been an act of rebellion on Ivy's part, and she was exhausted with the effort. Without another word, Ivy drifted into the wall.

Left alone, Alice stared at the closed door on the second floor and pondered Ivy's last word. *DON'T.* Perhaps Ivy had meant *Don't go into the room.* Or perhaps Ivy was reminding her, *Don't forget your promise to us.* It was hard to be certain with ghosts. You would think they would be more transparent, but Alice was often left wondering.

Alice rested one hand on the beautifully carved banister and gently placed her foot on the first step.

Chapter 9

Alice could see that some of the steps were clearly rotted through. She would avoid those. But she knew that a step might look solid when it wasn't, and the only way to tell for sure would be to put her weight on it. If the step was in fact rotten, it would be too late to fix her mistake.

The first four stairs were creaky but held, but the fifth step cracked underneath her, a sharp, ear-splitting sound like a gunshot. Alice quickly leaped onto the sixth step, which groaned but didn't give way. She could feel the whole staircase shift under her.

Then she heard a noise from above, not from the second floor, but higher up, perhaps the attic, which would have been the servants' quarters. There was a loud bang, followed by a clattering and then a muffled thud, as if something had been hurled against a wall and fallen to the floor.

Was it really Danny? wondered Alice. She couldn't imagine his droopy, melancholy mist making that kind of noise.

Alice continued to creep upstairs, carefully testing each step as she went. The hair on the back of her neck began to rise, as if the atmosphere was supercharged. Something unseen was in the air. Something that was angry and agitated.

There was another dull thud from above.

Alice placed her foot on the last step at the top of the long staircase. She shifted her weight forward. There was a creak, but it was no worse than the others.

Suddenly, a hole opened up beneath her big enough for Alice's entire body to slip through. Before she could understand what had happened, she was falling. She clawed her arms through the air and kicked her legs, hoping to grab on to something that might save her, but there was nothing within reach.

Just before she would have hit the floor, the front door blew open with so much force that the glass in a nearby window shattered. A tremendous tornado of wind blew through the house, a funnel of energy strong enough to lift Alice and hold her aloft. Instead of smashing onto the tiles, she landed as gently as a leaf settling on a lawn.

Alice lay still on the cold, dirty floor, thankful that she was unharmed. The cyclone of wind that had saved her from death swirled out of the House, and all was quiet.

"Okay, I get it!" she shouted. "You don't want me to go upstairs."

But inside her head, where she hoped her thoughts were still private, she was already thinking about how she might find a way into Danny's old room. And wondering about what was making those crashing sounds in the attic. Things could be hidden, it was true, but there were always ways to uncover them.

The next day, late in the afternoon, Alice was surprised when she looked up from her work to find Mugwort hovering in the parlor, reading a vaporous newspaper.

"Mugwort, how do you have a newspaper?" asked Alice.

Mugwort didn't look up. "I was reading this broadsheet when I died. Sometimes an object travels with us. Ivy's valise. Danny's locket."

"Danny's locket?" asked Alice, perking up.

"*Don't* ask him about it," warned Mugwort. "He will commence to keen, and my head will literally *fall off.*" Mugwort turned a page, and the newspaper dissolved and reformed in his hands.

Alice opened her mouth, but then decided to wait. Questions irritated Mugwort, and he seemed particularly gravelly today.

"I read your book at the library," said Alice. "It said very nice things about you."

"We fought and won at the Battle of Saratoga," said Mugwort wearily. "We lost with honor at the Battle of Brandywine."

"You did. It's all in the book," said Alice. "The thing is . . ." Alice cleared her throat. "The book is kind of *old*."

"Adam's ale!" said Mugwort, looking up for the first time since she entered the room. "It was written in the *twentieth* century. The twentieth century! It's so modern, it's nearly vulgar."

Alice held her tongue. She had learned from Ivy that it was no use trying to explain *time* to one who was Past Due. For them, all of forever was held in an instant, and a single moment could last ten lifetimes. She changed the subject. "Is Danny around?"

"Danny's always around," grumbled Mugwort. "Why do you think I'm out *here*? It's because he is in *there*. And he's in a fine and fettled mood today," he added sarcastically.

"Maybe I can get him out of the walls," said Alice.

Mugwort snorted. "Good luck, missy."

"A poem might bring him out. I know one by heart. My father taught it to me."

"Poetry!" Mugwort harrumphed. "It's of no use on the battlefield."

"Well, I'm going to try," said Alice.

Alice stood in the middle of the room.

*"Old Houses Speak
With words that time forgot*

They groan and creak,
And settle and weep
For long-lost children
That played in their yards."

She felt a dampness seep into the room and the temperature dropped several degrees. Danny was sitting in a corner of the parlor. Mugwort was gone.

"Hi, Danny," said Alice.

"I like that poem," said Danny. "It's very sad. The house is forgotten. The children are gone."

Alice frowned. "Mugwort's right," she said. "You *are* in a mood. Hey, I have a question. Do you have a locket?"

Danny's hand darted to his pocket. "You can't have it."

"I don't want it," said Alice matter-of-factly. "And even if I did, I couldn't take it. My hand would pass right through."

Danny fiddled with the thing in his pocket.

"I just want to see it," said Alice.

Danny bit his lower lip, causing the smoky outline of his mouth to disintegrate entirely. "All right, but only for a minute." He pulled out his hand to reveal a vaporous heart-shaped locket hanging on a wisp of a chain.

"Are there pictures inside?" asked Alice breathlessly. If she could *see* what Jenny had looked like, it might help Alice find her.

Danny unclasped the locket. Alice leaned in and tried as best she could to make out the features of the two small photographs pressed into the halves of the heart. The features kept shifting. The noses grew long, then short. The eyes drifted apart and came together. The mouths thinned and thickened, sometimes disappearing altogether. There was no way for Alice to see what Danny and Jenny had once looked like from these photos.

Danny closed the locket. "Long-lost children that played in their yards," he said lugubriously.

"Oh, Danny," said Alice. "Don't give up. I'll think of something."

In fact, the misty locket had already presented a thread of an idea to her. The photographs in the locket reminded her of something Professor Erasmus had mentioned—the library archives. Wouldn't there be copies of old yearbooks in the college library? Yearbooks are full of photographs, photographs of *every* student.

"I have to go," Alice said, but Danny had already begun to drift back into the walls. He gave no sign that he had even heard her.

"Mom?" asked Alice that evening as she snuggled with her mother under a quilt. They were both seated on the living room couch in front of the fireplace. There was no fire. The flue had caved in years ago. The fireplace reminded Alice of an empty eye socket, useless and ugly and dark.

"What, my little ibid?" asked her mother.

"Is there a Professor Gurkenstein who teaches at the college?"

"No," said her mother. "You must be thinking of Professor Gradensteif. He teaches in the Applied Mathematics Department. Brilliant, but phlegmatic."

Alice's father chimed in. "Is he the one who called our family an obtuse triangle because of our various heights?" He was balanced adroitly on a small stepladder, taping heavy plastic to the windows to try to make the room less drafty.

"Exactly!" said Alice's mother, sipping her tea. "*And* he meant it as a compliment! Why do you ask, Alice?"

"I was doing some research on someone who used to go to this college," said Alice. "I thought she might still be around." Actually, Alice's trip to the archives had been derailed when she encountered a posted sign on the front door of the college library that said it was closed "indefinitely" due to a "persistent and growing mouse problem."

"Some stay, some leave," acknowledged her mother, returning her attention to the scholarly journal she was reading. "I suppose that's always true of college towns. I stayed."

"And I came back!" said her father, stepping down from the ladder and sitting next to Alice on the couch.

Alice tugged and flapped the blanket so that it would cover her father's short legs. He had on two pairs of wool socks, but one of his toes still managed to poke through.

"You didn't go to college here," said Alice.

"No, but a branch of the Potchnik family settled in this town a *very* long time ago. Did I ever tell you about my great-great . . ." He looked to his wife quizzically: "One more *great*?"

"Yes," said Alice's mother, "great-great-*great*-aunt Zoya."

"Is she the one who hid in the root cellar?" asked Alice.

"No," answered her father.

"The one who was a pirate?"

"No."

"The one who played the violin for the king of Prussia?"

"No."

"The one who set fire to the village tree?"

"No."

"The one who had triplets, and then they all had triplets, and then they all had triplets?"

"No, no, no," said her father. "Great-Great-Great-Aunt Zoya . . . wait, we have a photograph." He started to push himself to his feet, then stopped to ask his wife, "Where are the photos, dearest?"

"Still in their boxes. In the basement. I hate to unpack them amidst all this wrack and ruin," said Professor Cannoli. "I'm afraid something will collapse on them!"

Her father paused. The basement was cold. The basement had spiders. And the basement lights didn't work. "Well," said her father, settling back onto the couch and burying his exposed toe beneath the quilt, "we have a photograph of her, and she decided to live in this town a long, long time ago, and when I was young and rambling, I came here to see if I still had any relatives in the area, descendants of Zoya, who was long gone at that point. I didn't find any. Instead, I found your mother." He reached across the back of the couch and took his wife's hand in his own. "Thank you, Great-Great-Great-Aunt Zoya, from the bottom of my heart."

Overhead, the light sizzled and zapped, and then it went out.

Alice's mother closed her journal and sighed. "Perhaps it's a sign that we should go to bed."

"Perhaps it's a sign that I should rewire the circuit board?" asked her father.

"Never!" said her mother.

"This house is a disaster!" said Alice.

"None of that!" said Professor Cannoli. "The Cannoli-Potchniks do not know the meaning of the word *surrender!*"

Alice's father leaned over and whispered in Alice's ear, "Maybe we should look it up in the dictionary." Alice giggled.

They gathered their books and blankets in the dark and began to march upstairs, single file.

"Wait!" Alice's mother stopped so suddenly on the dark staircase that Alice bumped into her mother and Alice's father bumped into Alice. Professor Cannoli tapped her chin. "There *is* someone named Gurkenstein." Alice's heart began to thump in her chest. "But not on faculty. A visiting fellow, I believe. Just arrived. In the Medieval Cultures Department. No. The Mathematics Department. No. Molecular Microbiology? I know it begins with an M . . ." She proceeded up the stairs, two at a time as she always did on account of her long legs, still tapping her chin as she went.

Music, Alice thought silently.

"Go on, Alice," whispered her father. "Teeth to brush and prayers to say. And besides, my toe is freezing!"

Alice ran up the stairs wishing she could hurry the night into day, wishing she could transform today into tomorrow. Perhaps tomorrow the library would be open. And perhaps a trip to the Music Department would reveal something about Danny's true love.

Jenny Gurkenstein, thought Alice as she climbed into bed, *you can't hide forever.*

Chapter 10

Alice left her house the next morning before her parents were even up and was waiting on the front steps of the college library when Mrs. Fein arrived. The mouse problem was not entirely solved, but there had been "some progress." Alice didn't ask any questions.

She located the college yearbook from 1972 and quickly found Danny's senior picture. *Charles Lowell.* The senior photos were labeled with names, but all the candid photos—of clubs and outings and eating in the dining hall—had funny captions that didn't list the people in the pictures. Alice thought this was kind of sloppy of the yearbook staff. It was also frustrating because there was no mention of Jenny

Gurkenstein anywhere in the 1972 yearbook.

Alice retrieved the yearbooks from 1969 to 1975 and carefully examined *every* senior portrait. No Jenny Gurkenstein had graduated from the college during those seven years.

There was one clue, however. At least Alice thought it might be a clue. In one of the candid photographs, labeled "The Cool Coders of the Computer Club," there was a picture of Danny staring at a young woman who was looking into the camera lens. The woman had a pretty smile with a slightly crooked front tooth and a long ponytail that reached all the way to her waist. Alice looked carefully at the expression on Danny's face and thought, *That's the way Dad looks at Mom. Love.*

Alice wanted to show the photograph to Danny, but the yearbook was a reference book, and reference books didn't circulate. Then again, neither did Danny. The yearbook couldn't leave the college library, and Danny wouldn't leave the House.

"Mrs. Fein?" asked Alice, approaching the librarian's desk with the yearbook in her hand.

"Alice," said Mrs. Fein, tapping her computer monitor. "Your name popped up on my screen this morning. You still haven't returned *Images of American Living: Three Centuries of Domestic Architecture.* Have you lost it?"

"Oh no, Mrs. Fein," said Alice, thinking how safe the book was, tucked under the porch where no one would ever find it. "I'll bring it back. I promise. But for now . . . I know that reference books can't be checked out, but could you please make an exception? I only need the book for a couple of hours, and I promise I'll bring it right back. In perfect condition. I'll guard it with my life."

Mrs. Fein looked truly sorry, but resolute. "I wish I could, Alice, but no reference books are *ever* allowed to leave the library. They're irreplaceable."

Both Alice and Mrs. Fein turned to look at the photocopy machine, which displayed its usual Out of Order sign. Mrs. Fein repeated, "I wish I could." And then without turning her head, she raised her voice and said loudly, "No feet on the furniture, please!" and Alice watched as a student behind Mrs. Fein shifted his feet off the table where they'd been resting. *Her antennae!* thought Alice. *She senses everything!*

Alice wandered back to the reference shelf. If Danny could tell her that the woman in the photograph was Jenny, then Alice would recognize her when she visited the Music Department.

The shelf where the book belonged was across the room from the circulation desk and completely hidden from its view. But what did that matter? Mrs. Fein could see without seeing and hear without hearing. Alice was sure of it.

Slowly, Alice began to slip the book into her canvas bag when she heard Mrs. Fein call out. "Alice? Is everything okay back there?" Alice froze with the book in her hand.

"Fine, Mrs. Fein! Everything's fine!"

"I'll come and help you put the book back. It's on a high shelf, I know." There was a brief pause, and then she called out more loudly, "Stop chewing gum on the third floor. There's no gum allowed in the library!"

The situation was hopeless.

Alice felt a sudden coolness around her, as if she had opened a refrigerator door. She looked up from the shelf. At first, she thought it might be Ivy, but then she sensed a grumbling in her bones. "Mugwort?"

There was no answer. Alice knew that the Blessing of the House didn't extend all the way to the college library. As powerful as the House was on its own ground, it had no powers here.

"Did you come to look at your book?" asked Alice. A dampness settled on her shoulders and formed a drop of moisture on the tip of her nose. She hoped that he would assume the book was checked out when he saw that it was missing.

"Mugwort, I need your help!" said Alice. "Can you . . . dampen . . . someone's senses? I mean, if you, I don't know, *enshrouded* someone with your mist, could that fog them up so that they wouldn't notice something else that was going on across the room?"

Alice felt a sudden shock wave in her bones. Mugwort was insulted. She realized too late that she had called his "essence" a "mist." She had explicitly called him "damp." And as if that weren't bad enough, she had suggested he "fog up" a human, which Mugwort would find absolutely revolting.

"I'm sorry, I'm sorry," she whispered, "but I really need your help. If you could go over to that woman behind the desk and just *confuse her*, it would be such a huge help. It would be *heroic*."

The dampness around her seemed to swirl, and then it disappeared. Either Mugwort was helping her or he had abandoned her. Time would tell.

Slowly but purposefully, Alice slipped the yearbook into her bag. She walked from behind the shelves and past the circulation desk where Mrs. Fein sat staring off into the distance as if lost in a dream. As always, the security gate, which was supposed to sound an alarm if someone tried to take a book without checking it out, wasn't working. She hurried out the door. "Thank you, Mugwort," she whispered as she headed for the House.

Alice had been working for less than an hour sanding the woodwork around one of the floor-to-ceiling windows when she noticed a puddle in the middle of the floor.

"Oh, Danny!" she said sympathetically, putting down her sanding block. "Can you pull yourself together?"

Droplets of rain began to fall up from the puddle until Danny's misty form appeared.

"I have something I want to show you," said Alice, walking to her canvas tote bag. The melancholy ghost drifted over to the window, as if he hadn't even heard her. She picked up the heavy yearbook and said, "There are pictures of you in here, when you were living."

Danny continued to look out the window, unmoved.

"There are also pictures of *her*," said Alice.

Danny transported so quickly across the room that he completely disorganized. His lower half got left behind while his upper half rushed forward. When both parts caught up, his body ran into the wall, and little rivulets trickled down the newly painted surface.

"Hey!" said Alice. "I spent a week painting that wall."

Danny reformed, and Alice showed him the senior portrait. "That's you. Charles Lowell."

Danny peered at the photograph. "I don't remember him at all," he said. "A complete stranger."

Alice turned to a different page. "Do you remember anyone in this photograph?" Alice held her breath.

Danny's outline wobbled. "That's Jenny." He pressed his misty eyeball within inches of the photograph of the woman with the crooked tooth.

"Are you sure?" asked Alice excitedly.

"Positive," he said. "We used to write code together. The college had three terminals and a limited number of punch cards—"

"What are punch cards?" asked Alice.

"You write code on the terminal and then it punches holes in a card so that you can feed the card into the teletype, which sends the code to the mainframe. Don't you know anything about computers?"

Alice had to hold herself back from explaining to Danny how computers work today. She simply said, "You should get out of the walls more, Danny. Really."

"It's so strange to think," he said, "I could have been part of the future." He stared once more at the photo of Jenny. "May I keep that?"

Alice shook her head. "It's a library book, but I can get you a scan."

"A what?"

"Never mind. I need to go. The Music Department's office hours start at ten, and I don't want to be late."

On her way to the Music Department, Alice stopped at the college library and handed the 1972 yearbook to Mrs. Fein.

"I'm very sorry I took it after you told me not to. I can truly say it was a matter of life or death, but it was still the wrong thing to do." Alice pondered this conundrum: She knew it was wrong to take the book, but she also knew she would do it again in the same circumstances. How could she make sense of that?

Mrs. Fein was not pleased. She gave Alice a stern lecture about how no one, *not even herself*, was above the laws of the library. She sentenced Alice to shelve books for an hour every Monday for the rest of the semester. Alice wondered if Mrs. Fein knew that shelving books was something Alice enjoyed; she thought she saw the tiniest of smiles on Mrs. Fein's face.

Alice jumped back on her bicycle and headed across the

college green. The Music Department clung to the edge of campus, housed in a fake Greek Revival house with stout Doric columns guarding the crooked door. As Alice climbed the steps of the dubious porch, the door swung open and out walked Professor Plim.

"Alice!" she shrieked. Professor Plim almost always shrieked. "Dear Alice! I haven't seen you in forever. Look at you, growing before my eyes. There! There! I swear you just grew another inch, *right before my eyes*!"

"Hello, Professor Plim," said Alice, as Professor Plim scooped up both of Alice's hands and held them close to her heart. She had a way of making everyone feel like they were the dearest person on earth to her.

"How is your mother? I adore your mother! And your father? How is the new house? Oh, your father will turn it into a palace in no time. The man has the genius and skill of a Michelangelo. You must all come to my house for coffee and sticky buns! Yes! I will send a note to your mother through the campus mail. Coffee and sticky buns! The answer to every problem of the heart!"

Alice stopped short, her hands still held in Professor Plim's plump embrace. "What do you mean . . . a problem of the heart?"

"Just an expression of my devout belief," said Professor Plim, "that sticky buns are truly the correct answer to every question."

Alice liked sticky buns quite a bit, but she was determined to stay focused on her mission. "I have a question," said Alice. "Is there a visiting fellow at the Music Department named Professor Gurkenstein?"

Professor Plim gave Alice a wry smile. "Now, Alice, when was the last time this college had money for the Music Department? We haven't had so much as a visiting bassoonist in over a decade. No, I'm afraid music isn't 'trendy' enough to get the big bucks. The future, dear Alice, lies that way." She inclined her head, and Alice followed her gaze across the college green to a small but distinctive cube of concrete that was snuggled between the Biology Department and Economics building. "They just finished it this summer. It's a brutal thing, don't you think?"

Alice agreed that the building was severe—all hard angles, straight lines, and blank surfaces. There was no elegance to it, but there were also no lies. It was what it was, without apology. Alice could accept that.

"What is it?" asked Alice.

"Something new," said Professor Plim. "The Department of Modern Culture and Media. Whatever that means. The future!" She looked at her watch. "I must fly!" Alice really did believe that Professor Plim had the energy and optimism to take wing. "Say hello to your mom and dad for me, and don't forget: sticky buns!"

Professor Plim trundled down the sidewalk, already

shrieking hello to the next person she met. Alice stared across the green lawn at the hulking cement building. "Modern Culture and Media," she said quietly to herself. "M and M."

Inside, the Modern Culture and Media building was surprisingly pleasant, though everything was made of heavy gray concrete. The floors were concrete; the walls and ceiling were concrete, even the reception desk and waiting bench were concrete. Yet the building had the feeling of a safe resting place, and it was comfortingly warm inside. The smooth, unvarying emptiness made Alice feel as though her heart rate could slow down, and her body felt solidly rooted in the ground. She remembered what Ivy had said about stone: how it is the source of strength and knowledge for any building that rests on it. She also remembered what her mother had said about permanence and how it was a stabilizing force. Alice could feel the sense of calm that radiated from this unmovable building.

There was no one at the reception desk, and Alice was so accustomed to going where her curiosity led her that she didn't hesitate to descend the stairs.

On the lower level, which was belowground, she found a black box theater and a row of closed doors, each with a neat metal nameplate: M. Lockhart, T. Espinoza, and a particularly mysterious one labeled simply *e*.

On the very last door, there was a torn index card. It was taped crookedly where a nameplate should have been, and the card announced in a sloppy scrawl, J. GURKENSTEIN.

Alice's heart began to pound. Was it really her? She knocked on the door.

"Yes!" shouted a voice as if it were answering all the questions of the universe in the affirmative.

Alice opened the door.

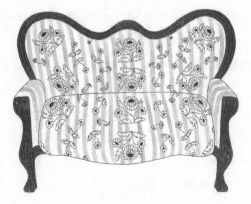

Chapter 11

The windowless concrete office was mostly empty, and everything about it shouted the word *temporary*. In the center of the room was a desk, and seated at the desk was a woman dressed all in black, with a single silver braid that reached to her waist. She wore a bright red slash of lipstick, and dark eyeliner rimmed her eyes. Two oversized silver hoops hung from her ears, framing the high cheekbones of her elegant face. She could have been anywhere from sixty to eighty years old.

Alice knew: It was her. The years had changed her, but not enough.

Alice stood silently in the doorway, stunned that she had actually found the woman that Danny had been in love with for almost fifty years. The woman looked up at Alice with great kindness. "Is there something I can do for you?" Alice saw the lovely crooked tooth.

Alice couldn't think of a single reason for being there—at least not one that anyone would believe.

"Are you lost?" the woman asked. Alice stared at the decorative plant on Professor Gurkenstein's desk. It still had a bow and a card tucked into it, no doubt a welcome gift from the department head. Alice had no skill with growing things, but even she could see that the plant was suffering, no doubt from a lack of natural light. She predicted it would be dead before the end of the term.

Alice shook her head, still unable to find any useful words.

"Well." Professor Gurkenstein seemed at a loss. "Do you want to sit down?"

Alice sat in the solitary chair reserved for students during office hours. She imagined that very few students would make their way down to this cryptlike office at the end of the hall.

Suddenly, Alice felt a wave of coldness pass through her that left the bangs on her forehead damp, and she knew that she and Professor Gurkenstein were no longer alone. But *who* had wafted in? Alice peered into the corners, but no mist organized itself into any kind of form. Instead, the whole room seemed filled with thin, foglike cobwebs.

"*Oof da!*" said Professor Gurkenstein, pulling a stylish cashmere shawl over her shoulders. "Is it me or is this office *cold*?" She returned her gaze to Alice. "You have an intelligent look in your eyes, but if you can't tell me why you're here, I'm going to have to assume you're a lost child and call security. I don't know much about children, and I would need help in figuring out what to do."

"I'm not," said Alice. "I . . ." But words failed her. She had not gamed out this part of the plan, because she hadn't truly believed that she would find Jenny. What could she do? The Cannoli side of her family told her, *Review the data!* The Potchnik side shouted, *Improvise!*

"Yes?" said Professor Gurkenstein, leaning forward.

"I'm actually Professor Cannoli's daughter, in the Anthropology Department."

"Oh! I've heard of your mother," said Professor Gurkenstein. "I'm told she's the best lecturer on campus. I'm looking forward to sitting in on one of her classes."

Alice watched as the fog began to coalesce. It was gathering in a thick ball, gray and stormy, just over Professor Gurkenstein's left shoulder. Inside the vaporous sphere, Alice could see that tears were beginning to fall.

"Danny . . ." she whispered, wishing she could comfort him. This must be terribly hard on him, and he was so prone to melancholy, even on his best days.

"I'm sorry?" said Professor Gurkenstein. "Did you say Charlie?"

Alice was caught off-guard. She stared at the weeping cloud. "Yes. Yes, that *is* what I said."

"How strange. I was just thinking about . . . Do you know

I went to this college? I didn't graduate here. I left because, well . . . there was some sadness, and I couldn't stay. I had a very good friend here named Charlie. A long time ago." She stared at the papers on her desk with a half smile on her face, unaware of the storm cloud gathering behind her. "He used to make me *laugh*. You're too young to understand this, but remember it for the future: Hold on to the ones who make you laugh."

"It sounds like you loved him," said Alice boldly. "Maybe he loved you, too." The thick gray ball of mist was beginning to drip water onto the floor.

"Charlie?" said Professor Gurkenstein, her eyebrows raised in surprise. "Oh no. Charlie never felt that way about me. He was a senior and I was just a freshman. To him I was a friend, nothing more."

There was a loud sound like the crack of thunder, and the thick and murky mist pushed itself through the ceiling, scattering drops as it disappeared.

"Is it raining outside? And is it *leaking* in here?" asked Professor Gurkenstein. She looked up at the ceiling. "I thought this was a new building."

"But what if I told you that he did?" asked Alice. "What if I could prove to you that he loved you?"

Professor Gurkenstein looked at her. "What *is* your name?"

"Alice."

Professor Gurkenstein looked at Alice with a warm and sympathetic smile. "Alice. You really do have a face that seems wise beyond your years. But trust me. Charlie Lowell was *not* in love with me. And there's *nothing* you could do to convince me otherwise."

A burst of water sprayed onto Professor Gurkenstein's desk, covering her papers and the drooping plant.

"What in heaven's . . . ?" exclaimed Professor Gurkenstein. "This building—"

"Then why were you thinking about him?" persisted Alice.

"I suppose coming back here has reminded me of a lot of things," Professor Gurkenstein said. She looked intensely at Alice. "Do you ever feel haunted by ghosts?"

"What?" Alice gripped her chair to keep from jumping out of it.

"I mean *metaphorically*. Ghosts from the past. I've felt this way for years. Maybe because of how I left, it's as if my time here was unfinished somehow," said Professor Gurkenstein. "When they offered me the visiting fellowship, I should have said no. It's a *terrible* career move, but I couldn't." She stared at the brutal cement wall. "It's like something was drawing me here."

The House, Alice thought. And suddenly Alice could see Professor Gurkenstein's fate. She, too, had neglected to tell someone she loved him, and when she died, she would become one of the Past Due. Had the House drawn her here? Or perhaps she'd felt the heavy sway of this unforgiving concrete building. Alice knew that trees talk to each other underground over vast and dense networks. Perhaps buildings could communicate with each other through the bedrock of the earth.

"I'm not sure it was a good idea for me to come back," said Professor Gurkenstein. She shrugged and pulled the cashmere shawl more tightly around her shoulders, curling into the back of her chair. "So many memories. I feel like I'm surrounded by ghosts." She stared at the plant, then sat up straight. "Is it my imagination, or does that plant look like it's about to keel over dead?"

It's true, the plant seemed barely able to support itself, and it had dropped a dozen leaves in the time since Alice had arrived.

"It's the melancholy," sighed Alice. "It brings everyone down."

"Have you been haunting her for years?" Alice accused Danny once they were both back at the House.

"No!" said Danny, flattened like a pancake against the parlor wall so that his essence reached from floor to ceiling. "This is the first time I ever left the House since I died. I was just following *you*, and then you ended up *there*."

"She said she's been feeling haunted for a long time."

"It could have been anyone," said Ivy. "Different spirits haunt people for lots of reasons. And some living humans are much more hauntable than others. They're practically haunting magnets. She might be one of those."

"I haunted my children," said Mugwort. "I had seven of

them. I wanted to see how they turned out." He smiled over his newspaper. "Settled, every one of them."

"Well, stay away from Jenny Gurkenstein. And her dying plant!" said Alice sternly. "All of you. She already had a look in her eyes like she might bolt. And we need her to stay around so that I can convince her that Danny loved her—which I have no idea how I'm going to do. But at least she's *here*. We need to keep it that way, because there isn't enough garage-sale money for me to be chasing her all over the country!"

The sofa arrived, and it was just as Roberta had promised, spectacular beyond belief. Deep in the fabric bins of the Theater Arts Department, Roberta had found a gorgeous yellow silk brocade with green stripes and hand-embroidered floral details. She had cleaned it and steamed it and cut the fabric so expertly that there was just enough to cover the carved wooden frame.

Alice wrestled the sofa into the parlor. She could feel Ivy's cool breath on the back of her neck and hear a sigh of contentment.

"Oh, Alice," said Ivy. "It's lovely!"

"Roberta did a great job," agreed Alice.

"Not just the sofa. The whole room. Look at all the work you've done."

And for the first time, Alice really did step back and look at the room, not just at each piece of the repairwork she'd done: the fireplace and the chandelier and the walls and the curtains. She looked at it all together and saw that she had done good work. The Potchnik in her was proud. The Cannoli in her said, *"Bravissimo!"*

"It looks the way it used to," said Ivy with satisfaction. "I feel like I'm *home*." She floated up in the air and then settled on the beautiful sofa, her valise placed carefully at her side. "It feels so good to come home."

Alice could feel it too. Perhaps not in the same way as Ivy, who had actually lived in the House, but she had a sense of what it meant to return to a place and to feel happy and secure and welcomed inside.

The thought occurred to Alice in the middle of the night. The next morning, she hurried through breakfast and then rushed to the House.

Ivy was draped over the chandelier, looking like she'd had a very rough night. Mugwort was wedged under the staircase.

"We can't take it anymore," said Ivy. "The constant wailing. The screaming. The tearing out of his hair—which just grows back so he can tear it out some more. It's even worse than before! Mugwort and I have been out of the walls all night, and that's not restful for our essences. I am coming undone!"

It was true. Ivy's legs were drooping to twice their normal length and looked like they might simply fall off her body.

"I need to see Danny," said Alice.

"You won't get him out," snapped Mugwort. His nose had

drifted over to where his left ear should have been. Both eyes were dripping down his cheeks like runny eggs that hadn't been allowed to cook long enough. "He has flattened himself to the thinness of an onion skin and spread his essence *all over* the inside of the walls. He's everywhere! A job well done, Miss Bossy Flossy! Taking him to see that woman!"

"I didn't take him!" said Alice. "He followed me!"

"You should have anticipated! God's bones! This is serious business. I'm exhausted! If we can't get him out with all reasonable haste, I'm going to *dissipate* until I become one of the Forever Forgotten!"

"But I have an idea," said Alice. "We need to find his poems."

"To what end?" asked Mugwort. "And what about me? What about *my* Unfinished Business? You've hardly paid any attention to it at all."

"I *am* working on it," said Alice, "I promise. It's just taking some time."

"Folderol!" shouted Mugwort. "My head is splitting in two!" And Alice saw that it was literally true: Mugwort's head was cleaving right down the middle.

Alice took a piece of paper out of her pocket and started to read in a quiet, soothing voice.

"Two roads diverged in a yellow wood . . ."

Alice waited, listening, then continued.

"And sorry I could not travel both
And be one traveler, long I stood . . ."

She paused again. For a moment, she thought she saw a mist rising from behind the painting of the storm-tossed ship. The mist, however, dissolved into nothingness.

"And looked down one as far as I could
To where it bent in the undergrowth."

"Enough!" shouted Mugwort, standing up. "He is *here*, and I am gone." Mugwort marched straight into the wall and disappeared.

Alice looked up and saw that a cloud of rain had gathered around the chandelier. She held her breath and watched as Danny rained down into the room.

Chapter 12

"I can't bear it," said Danny. "I've told the House that I'm going to seep into the floor of the basement and stay there until the last person who knew me on earth is gone. Then I'll become one of the Forever Forgotten. They have no memories at all. I'd rather have no memories than these."

"No, Danny!" said Alice, but Ivy perked up as if she thought this might not be a bad idea.

Alice continued. "You have to fight. You have to try to remember *more*. Where did you put the poems you wrote to Jenny?"

"I don't know."

"Try!"

"I know they're safe. I put them somewhere safe." Danny sank onto the sofa, as if the burden of holding up his weightless vapor was too much.

"But *where*?" implored Alice.

"Someplace dark," said Danny, pressing the heels of his palms into his eye sockets.

"A closet?" asked Alice.

"A grave?" asked Ivy.

"No," said Danny. "Warm. And dry. And . . . noisy."

"Noisy?" asked Ivy.

"What kind of noise?" asked Alice.

"A . . ." Danny dropped his hands and closed his transparent eyelids. "A squeak."

Alice and Ivy looked at him.

"Oh no!" said Alice, suddenly understanding. A squeak. Mice! The *sofa*! It was warm and dry and dark inside the cushions, and mice had been living in there for years. "Danny, did you stuff the poems inside the cushions of the sofa?"

"Maybe. I don't remember."

"It's a very good place to hide something," said Ivy. She turned to Alice. "Are you going to tear it open?"

"It won't do any good," said Alice. "Roberta threw out all the old stuffing. She said it was unsanitary because of the mouse droppings. She bagged it all up and took it to the dump. It's gone."

They all stared at the beautiful, good-as-new sofa and thought about what they had lost. Alice knew she couldn't help Danny without the poems. She sat down on the floor and put her head in her hands.

"Not in the couch," muttered Danny, shaking his head.

Alice looked up.

"Not in the couch," said Danny again. "I can see the poems, but they're not in the stuffing of the couch. There's a poem I know."

"This isn't the time to recite a poem, Danny," said Ivy. She was so exhausted, even her valise dripped to the floor.

"This poem is different. This poem is the key. I recited it every day to remind myself where I'd hidden the poems, because Ivy told me I would forget everything. But I've always remembered poetry. So I made the poem the key to where I'd hidden the other poems. I kept reciting it all the time, until . . . I forgot about reciting it."

"You can remember, Danny," said Alice, standing up. "I know you can."

Ivy flew to Danny's side and laid a ghostly hand on his shoulder. "Try, Danny. You can do it."

Even Mugwort, who had crept out of the walls, stood at attention and said, "Rally, sir, rally! Give it your best shot."

"A mouse . . . and something . . . the warmth," Danny muttered to himself. He started to rise in the air, as if the act of concentrating was inflating him. "*Under the* . . . I know that's how it begins. *Under the* . . ." He shook his head and dropped to the ground. "I can't remember."

"Say it with me," said Alice encouragingly. "Under the

something, there once was a mouse . . ."

"No!" Danny's form suddenly grew tall, shooting up until his head reached the ceiling. "*Under the floorboard that squeaks like a mouse . . .*"

"Okay!" said Alice excitedly. "Under the floorboard that squeaks like a mouse . . . That's good, Danny. What's next?"

Danny collapsed to his usual size and began to drift back and forth in the small parlor.

"I know you can do this, Danny. Think. What rhymes with *mouse*?"

"*Louse*," offered Mugwort.

"*Blouse*!" shouted Ivy.

"*House*," whispered Alice.

"*House*!" said Danny. "I remember."

"*Under the floorboard that squeaks like a mouse,*
And close to the warmth that's the heart of the House."

"The heart of the House," said Alice. "Everyone knows . . ."

Danny, Ivy, Mugwort, and Alice all turned to look at the fireplace.

"There's a floorboard that always squeaks when I step on it," said Alice. She hurried to the fireplace and then stepped on each board to find the one that squeaked. It was right in the center, directly under the heart tile.

Alice kneeled down. She pressed on one end of the squeaky floorboard and the other end rose up. "It isn't even nailed in place!" she said. She removed the board and shined her pocket flashlight into the space beneath the floor. There was a large envelope stuffed between the joists. She reached down and pulled the envelope out.

"Those are my poems," Danny said. "I put all my heart into them when I was alive."

Alice's hands trembled as she reached into the envelope and retrieved a stack of cards. They were made of thin cardboard, and each one was punched through with precise holes. The cards reminded her of train tickets punched by a conductor to mark a final destination. Alice turned over the first card, and then the second.

"Danny? There aren't any words on these."

"I didn't want anyone reading them. So I put them all in code. But it's simple. You just run the cards through the tele-type to print them out on paper."

"What's a teletype?" asked Alice.

"A teletype. You know. It hooks up to the campus main-frame. The big computer. The teletype is the terminal. You feed the punch cards into the teletype, and it sends the bits and bytes on the punch card to the mainframe and then, in about an hour, you get your printout. Unless the mainframe is backed up. Sometimes it takes days to get the printout."

"Danny!" said Alice, the color flowing out of her face. "These things you're talking about . . . mainframes . . . and terminals . . . and teletypes . . . they don't exist anymore. That's not how computers work these days. A lot has changed in the last fifty years. People have laptops. Or tablets. Or phones. Or watches. You can carry a computer in a ring on your finger!"

"That's ridiculous!" said Danny. "Computers are the size of houses!"

"Not anymore," said Alice in despair.

"You would have known that if you hadn't gone into the walls, Danny!" said Ivy. "If you'd gone out in the world, the way Mugwort and I do. All the kids at school have laptops. They don't even print out their papers anymore! They just send them to the teacher over WiFi."

"What's WiFi?"

"It's how you send things over the internet!" Ivy had watched plenty of living humans use their computers. "Oh! Don't even tell me you don't know what the internet is!"

"Danny," said Alice carefully, recovering from her disappointment at realizing that all they had was some useless cardboard cards with holes punched in them. "Can you remember the poems?"

"No! I carefully wrote them down in computer code. They're all right there—in your hand!" Danny started to storm. Bit by bit, his essence began to froth and churn.

"Don't worry," said Alice. "There has to be a way. Give me some time to think." The Cannoli-Potchnik in her was certain she would figure something out, but part of her worried that there was no solution to this puzzle.

Alice turned to Mugwort. "In the meanwhile, Mugwort, you'll be glad to hear I have a plan to help *you*."

"It's about time!" he said indignantly.

"But I need all of you—*all of you*—to come to the library with me. This is going to take everything we've got. And Mugwort, I can guarantee you're going to find the whole thing disgusting."

"Who's in the back corner?" called out Mrs. Fein.

"It's just me, Mrs. Fein! Alice! No worries!"

Alice was crouched behind a bookshelf in the corner farthest from the circulation desk. "You see what I mean?" she whispered to Ivy, Mugwort, and Danny. "She knows everything that's going on in the library. We're going to need a *big* distraction."

Alice couldn't see or hear any of the ghosts; they were beyond the reach of the House. She could, however, see occasional wisps of their essences, vining and trailing around the books, dripping and pooling on the shelves.

Alice balanced a final cube of gouda cheese on a heavy book. "Okay. Let's just go through this one more time. This book is balanced right on the edge of the shelf, ready to fall. All it needs is the smallest bit of weight to tip it over and send it crashing to the floor. None of you can move anything, so we need something—a mouse—to provide the weight. That means you *all* need to carry the smell of the cheese on your essences and spread it over the library, so that the mice will follow the scent trail back and tip over the book. I'll be up front talking with Mrs. Fein. When she goes to investigate the noise, I'll slip behind the circulation desk and grab Mugwort's book. Got it?"

There was no answer from the ghosts, but they had all talked it through back at the House. Mugwort had openly rebelled, insisting that *carrying an odor* was a humiliation he would not bear. "It's beyond the pale! The very idea! I was a highly decorated captain!"

"We're doing this for you, you stinky old gas bag!" Ivy had shouted.

"You senseless cub! You addle pate!"

"I'd rather stay home too," Danny had said, beginning to puddle. "Let's go back into the walls."

"No!" Alice had insisted. "We are doing this together."

Now that they were at the library, Alice was pretty sure the arguing and name-calling hadn't stopped. Spits of essence were lobbing themselves through the air, and little explosions of mist kept detonating. All she could do was hope that the ghosts would come through in the end.

At the circulation desk, Mrs. Fein was busy processing a pile of new books.

"Mrs. Fein," said Alice. "Do you ever worry that a mouse will just run across the desk and jump on you?"

"Never," said Mrs. Fein. "I can always tell where they are. Mice aren't stealthy enough to surprise me. And besides, all the mice are gone."

"Gone? How?"

"There are methods of persuasion," said Mrs. Fein obliquely.

"But I can say with certainty: There are no more mice in the library."

"Not one?" asked Alice, feeling faint.

"Not one. I can sense these things."

Oh no, thought Alice.

"What's that smell?" asked Mrs. Fein, a book held aloft in her hand.

"*Um,* I don't smell anything." The cheese smell was useless if there were no mice in the library.

"It's cheese!" said Mrs. Fein, horrified. She sniffed the air. "Gouda! Where is that coming from? There's no eating allowed in the library!"

"Maybe you should go check!" said Alice helpfully, pointing in the direction of the back corner.

"It's everywhere," said Mrs. Fein, covering her nose with her hand. "It's like a giant cheese fog has descended on the entire library! We're going to have to close. Alice, you'll have to leave this minute and all the students, too."

"Leave?" shouted Alice, hoping her voice carried to wherever Ivy, Mugwort, and Danny were. "And NO MICE?"

As quickly as it had come, the smell of the cheese began to clear.

"I think it's going away," said Alice.

"What in heaven's name do you think made that stink?" asked Mrs. Fein.

"We'll never know," said Alice ruefully. Her plan had failed. There were no mice to help them out.

The galloping sound of multiple books crashing to the ground poured out from the back of the library.

"That sounded like a *lot* of books," said Alice, even more surprised than Mrs. Fein, who was already scurrying to investigate.

As soon as Mrs. Fein disappeared into the stacks, Alice sprinted behind the circulation desk and grabbed the slim book with the long title. She rushed through the broken security gate and bolted for the door.

I hope I'm being followed, thought Alice.

But when she got back to the House, Ivy and Mugwort were already waiting for her. "What happened?" asked Alice. "Did a *hundred* mice show up?"

"No! No!" said Ivy, bobbing in the air with uncontrolled excitement. "*We* did it. We *did* it!"

"Ugh," said Mugwort, floating prostrate in the air and looking as though he'd been flattened by a wrecking ball. "What I wouldn't give for a strong cup of hot spiced rum and a throat with which to drink it!"

"Where's Danny?" asked Alice.

"In the walls," squealed Ivy. "It's going to take a *week* for him to recover!"

"Recover from what?"

Mugwort groaned, but Ivy couldn't wait to tell the story.

"When we heard there were no mice in the library, *I* came up with a new plan. I thought if we all swirled our essences together, we would be strong enough to tip the book."

"And it worked?" asked Alice.

"No," said Ivy. "Not at all! We were just as weak as ever. Couldn't move a dust bunny. But then Mugwort called me a *flibbertigibbet*, so I called him a *corny-faced blunderbuss*, which he really didn't like because he's vain, and he called me a *fussy crow*, and I called him a *gollumpus*, and all this time Danny was wailing away, and somehow we created a tornado, and *that's* what blew down all the books!"

"I had no idea," said Alice.

"Neither did we!" said Ivy. "Which just goes to show: If you die long enough, you see everything."

Mugwort floated slowly over toward Alice, as if he'd been wounded on a battlefield. "Did you get it?" he asked wearily.

Alice pulled the book out of her tote bag and held it up.

"And what, pray tell, are you going to do with it?"

"That's the next thing I have to figure out," said Alice.

"Well. I am going into the walls," said Mugwort. "I stink of cheese, and I believe I still have some of Danny's essence stuck in my hair. I'm done in." And he disappeared.

Chapter 13

Professor Henkle wore oversized bow ties that drooped on both ends and expensive Italian loafers with wildly patterned socks. According to Alice's mother, "That's pretty much all you need to know about the man."

Actually, what bothered Professor Cannoli most about Professor Henkle was that he cared more about becoming a dean than he did about teaching his students. Professor Cannoli had no patience for anyone who didn't do their best, whether it was the person operating the drive-thru car wash or the president of the United States. "Everyone has the responsibility to *try* to be excellent," she would say.

Alice's appointment with Professor Henkle, which had required three separate phone calls to schedule, was at four o'clock. But at 4:15, Alice was still sitting in the hallway outside his closed door. She assumed he was dealing with an important crisis with one of his students or a faculty member, because she could hear him talking with great vigor on the phone. However, when he finally allowed her in, she saw that his computer screen displayed an "Order Complete!" message from the Bow Tie Club. Apparently he had been shopping online. Alice also noticed a catalog for socks open on his desk, next to a tall pile of manuscripts. The manuscripts looked crisp and untouched, whereas the pages of the catalog had many folded-down corners.

Their brief meeting could be summarized thusly:

No, he was not interested in reading a book about prominent local citizens.

No, he had never heard of Captain Nathaniel Finch.

No, he wasn't interested in speaking about Captain Finch at any upcoming history conferences.

No, he didn't think the book *Millbrook, with Interest* would be a valuable addition to his personal library.

No, there wasn't anything he could do to help her.

"I simply don't have time," he explained, his gaze drifting once again to the glossy photographs of colorful socks.

"Well, thank you, I guess," said Alice, standing up from her chair. "You *are* an expert on the Revolutionary War, aren't you?" Perhaps she had mixed up Professor Henkle with another professor at the college—one who actually cared about scholarly work.

"Absolutely," he said. "It's my passion. I've written countless books on the subject"—he waved vaguely at the bookcase in his office—"and publishers from all over the country send me manuscripts for review." He pointed to the stack of unread manuscripts on his desk.

Alice read the title of the top one in the pile: "The Road to Independence."

"That's not a very good title," she said.

Professor Henkle sighed, as if it was hard to express how great a misfortune it was that he was required to read that particular book. "I have low expectations," he said.

"Can I look at the others?" asked Alice, reaching for the pile.

"No," he said coldly. "You are—" But just at that moment, the phone rang, and Professor Henkle turned his back on her to begin another spirited conversation with another customer service department about another online order that was not to his satisfaction.

Alice waited. It would be impolite to leave without saying a proper goodbye, and the Potchniks were very polite people. The Cannolis—not so much.

The Cannolis, however, *were* impossibly curious and could never resist a research opportunity when it presented itself. Alice kept her eyes on the back of Professor Henkle as she reached forward and began to flip through the manuscripts, reading each title. They did seem rather dull: "Conventional Military Formations During the Revolutionary War," "Lesser-Known Documents from the Time of the American Revolution," "Ordinary Farmers, Extraordinary Soldiers." Alice was more than halfway through the pile when she came upon one entitled "Scoundrels of the Revolutionary War: Profiteering in a Time of Independence."

Now, that's a great title, she thought, pulling the manuscript out of the stack. She sat down in the chair and began to read the introduction. Professor Henkle continued to argue.

"No! No! No! This is my point exactly. Just because brocade and jacquard look quite similar does *not* make them the same. Things are not always what they seem!"

Alice looked up. *Things are not always what they seem.* Something about the phrase caused an uneasy feeling in her stomach. She turned to the back of the manuscript and scanned the index under the letter F.

Faneuil Hall, 12, 18–21, 146
Farmers, loyal to the crown, 36–39
Farmers, Shays's Rebellion, 18, 42, 119, 220–32
Fay, Elizabeth, 79
Ferguson, Patrick, 110
Finch, Captain Nathaniel, 193–94

Alice's heart skipped a beat, and she had to work hard to swallow. She turned to page 193 and scanned the short entry, then closed the manuscript and placed it at the bottom of the pile on Professor Henkle's desk. She would not wait to say goodbye, even if it was impolite. Some things mattered more than politeness, and telling dear Mugwort the terrible truth of his Unfinished Business of the Heart was certainly one of those things.

"Alice!" shouted Professor Sosa from across the college green.

Alice was so deep in thought about Mugwort that she hadn't noticed Professor Sosa, himself struggling against the sharp, blustery wind. He taught in the Computer Science Department, and if it hadn't been for last year's faculty volleyball debacle, he would have been a regular dinner guest at the Cannoli-Potchnik table.

"Hi, Professor Sosa," said Alice, admiring his neat goatee and stylish glasses. "Any news?" A few days ago, Alice had given him Danny's computer punch cards, and he had offered to do a little digging on old computer technology.

"The best news," he said, a sly twinkle in his eyes. "My friend at the Living Computers Museum in Seattle received the punch cards you gave me. She said she tried to run one through their old teletype, which is still hooked up to a 1969 mainframe. Can you imagine?"

"And . . . ?" asked Alice, barely able to contain her excitement.

"Worked like a charm. Not a hitch. Smooth as silk. Right as rain!"

"It actually worked?" Alice hadn't even allowed herself to hope. The chances of deciphering fifty-year-old punch-card code had seemed impossibly slim.

"It did! Score one for simple technology. Punch cards!"

"So, when will I get the files?"

"My friend at the museum will run the cards tonight and then send the printouts to me, along with the punch cards. She assumed you would want those back? She said to tell you that the museum would pay a pretty penny to keep them for their collection."

"Let me think about that," said Alice, knowing she needed Danny's permission to sell the punch cards. Maybe with the money she could buy an antique clock for the mantelpiece of the House. Or maybe a rug! The money from the garage sale was almost gone. "Why can't she just send the files in an email?"

"Alice, those punch cards have to be processed by a very old computer and printed on a very old, continuous-feed printer. There's no conversion from a computer of that generation to any format we use today. But the printout should be ready tomorrow, as long as the printer doesn't break down. And then my friend will send it back overnight, and I'll call you the day after tomorrow—as soon as the package arrives," said Professor Sosa. "By the way, where did you find those old punch cards? They're rare, you know."

"Oh, we live in an old house," she said cheerfully. "And

I found the cards under some floorboards." Both statements were true; they just weren't connected.

"Marvelous!" said Professor Sosa. "Like an archaeologist. You're a credit to your mom and dad."

Alice wondered if that was true. Would all the subterfuge and sneaking around of the past few weeks make her parents proud? Or would they feel that they could trust her less? And did *she* trust *them*—to believe her and to allow her to help her friends in her own way? These were uncomfortable thoughts for Alice, who was accustomed to being in agreement with her parents.

I will tell them, she thought, *when the time is right*. But for the first time, she wondered if the time would ever be right. Would she ever want to share this magical part of her life— with anyone?

"Patience, Alice!" called out Professor Sosa as the wind blew him across the college green and toward the CS building. "All good things come to those who wait!"

"A profiteer?" whispered Ivy. "How awful!"

"*How* am I going to tell him?" asked Alice. "I spent hours last night trying to figure out the words to say. But I don't think I can!"

Alice had just finished telling Ivy what she had learned from the unpublished manuscript in Professor Henkle's office. The entire entry had been no more than two paragraphs—not the glorious full chapter in *Millbrook, with Interest* that Mugwort was so proud of. In "Scoundrels of the Revolutionary War," Captain Finch was only a minor character, but he had played his part. He had been a war profiteer, undiscovered during his lifetime but now exposed in this unpublished manuscript. During the war, he had diverted much of the gunpowder he manufactured—so desperately needed by the Continental Army to fight the British—to a company in Spain, and then sold it to the American colonies for five times its true cost. Like so many men of the time, all well known as Patriots, Captain Finch had made a fortune at the expense of the cause of liberty.

And yet, the unpublished manuscript pointed out that Captain Finch was a brilliant strategist and fearless commander, leading his men into battle time and again when he could have stayed safely at the rear of each assault. According to the book, his soldiers had been devoted to him. It mentioned the Battle of Brandywine, which was the longest single day of fighting in the war, and the Battle of Saratoga, which was a decisive turning point. By all accounts, Captain Finch had fought bravely at both. The manuscript made clear that Finch was both a devoted Patriot and someone who betrayed the cause to make himself rich. A complicated human.

"He has to know," said Ivy. "Or else he'll never be able to move on."

"But can't we somehow take care of his Unfinished Business

without him knowing?" Alice was mixed up in a lot of ways. She felt desperate to spare the old soldier's feelings, and she felt miserable knowing this truth about him. She almost wished she had never read that unpublished manuscript.

How could Mugwort have betrayed the soldiers he loved like brothers and sons?

Context! shouted her mother.

Complexity! explained her father.

"Mugwort?" called out Alice.

But he didn't show up, and Alice ended up spending the morning tearing up rotted floorboards. At two o'clock she rode her bike to a nearby salvage yard that sold all kinds of building materials from wreckages: houses and churches, grange halls and barns, ships and shops. She spent the entire afternoon poking through piles of reclaimed wood. When she returned to the House, it was shortly before sunset. She was happy because she'd found a good match for the floor in the parlor, frustrated because she didn't have the money to buy it, and worried because she knew she had to talk to Mugwort.

"My book," said a gravelly voice before Alice had even passed through the foyer. "Have you shown it to that Professer Whimple?"

Alice looked around the room. "Mugwort? Where are you?" She dropped her canvas tote bag on the floor.

"I'm in the walls," said Mugwort. "I feel as though I don't have the strength to advance."

"Well, Professor *Henkle* isn't going to be able to help us," admitted Alice. "But there's a new book with your name in it. It hasn't been published yet."

"A new book?" There was a hint of hope in his lifting voice, but he still sounded unbearably tired. "What is the title?"

Alice paused. "I don't think the title is particularly important," she said. "You see, the book says you did some bad things during the war, but *I* don't think that makes you a bad person."

"Bad things?" asked Mugwort, and Alice could hear the puzzlement in his voice, even though he was still hidden in the walls. "What bad things? We fought and won at the Battle of Saratoga. We lost with honor at the Battle of Brandywine . . ."

"Yes, you did," said Alice. "And the book mentions *all* of that. But you also made money from selling gunpowder to the Continental Army."

"Of course I did. That was my business, selling gunpowder. I had a manufactory. The army was desperate for gunpowder. Ammunition, horses, food, uniforms—all these things needed to be supplied by businesses. What kind of Patriot would I have been if I had refused gunpowder to my soldiers? If I had sent them into battle without the protection they needed?"

"Yes," said Alice. "But the book says . . ." She paused. "It says you sold the gunpowder for five times what it was worth. You took advantage of the army's desperation, and you made a lot of money by charging too much."

"Profiteering? Are you saying I was a profiteer?" His voice sounded more puzzled than angry.

"Maybe it's not true!" said Alice. "Maybe the historian got the facts wrong. I don't believe you're a scoundrel. You can't be."

Mugwort grew quiet—so quiet that Alice wondered if he had retreated. "I cannot say but what I know," he said at last. "I do not know that I was *not* a profiteer. Yet I know with complete certainty that the war was a terrible thing. And I emerged very rich. Rich enough to build this house."

There was a rumbling underneath Alice's feet.

"Also," said Mugwort slowly, "it explains the gold in the cellar."

A noisy *whoosh* of cold air tumbled down the staircase, rattling windows and lifting and swirling the autumn leaves that littered the floor of the foyer. Alice heard a door bang shut, and she could have sworn she heard the turning of a lock.

"Gold?" asked Alice.

"In the last stall in the cellar. I visit it often to settle my brain and quiet the thoughts that make riot therein. Each day I make sure the gold is there. I have forgotten from whence it came. I have forgotten why I stand guard over it."

Gold in the cellar? Alice had never expected the House to hold a secret like that.

She hurried down the hallway to the basement door, the same door she had come through on her first day in the House. She tried to turn the knob, but it was locked. She rattled it, yanking on the door.

"Hey!" she shouted to the House. "Unlock the door! If you

don't, I have the tools to pry it open."

One of the wooden chairs in the foyer leaped in the air and crashed to the floor, as if a tremendous force had knocked its legs out from under it. From somewhere upstairs came the sound of shattering glass.

"That doesn't impress me!" shouted Alice, although in truth, she *was* rather impressed by the House's display of force—and more than a little afraid of what might happen next. To give herself courage, she yelled, "Anything you can break, I can fix."

A piece of the staircase railing broke off and fell from the second story.

"Yep! I can fix that, too!" she called out. "You're not doing yourself any favors, you know. This is what my mother calls *cutting off your nose to spite your face*." In the silence, Alice sensed that the House was listening—and waiting. "Why don't you trust me?" whispered Alice, realizing that there was no need to shout. "I painted your walls. I sanded your wood-work. *I restored the heart tile*."

From thirty feet above, an enormous piece of the second-floor ceiling fell and shattered on the floor, spraying Alice with chunks of plaster and dust. In the stunned silence that followed, Alice heard the lock turn.

She descended the stairs quickly and found Mugwort waiting beside the last of the stalls that lined the wall. She remembered how she had looked in some of them on that first morning—but not this one.

She shined her pocket flashlight into the darkness of the bin and saw nothing. But when she climbed in, she stubbed her toe on a rusted iron ring that seemed attached to the dirt floor. Upon closer inspection, she saw that the ring was fastened to a small wooden door, no bigger than a sheet of notebook paper. She pulled on the iron ring and the door opened onto a dug-out space in which there was a wooden box the size of a small loaf of bread. It was hard to pull out the box because it was so heavy.

"Open it," said Mugwort.

Alice lifted the lid and shined her flashlight. Dozens of gold coins glittered in the bright beam.

"Spanish doubloons," said Mugwort. "The safest currency during the war. Never could I have earned such a tremendous fortune honestly."

Alice tried to put a hand on Mugwort's arm, but of course it was impossible. Her hand simply passed through him, leaving her palm damp and chilled. "We all make mistakes, Mugwort. You're a good person."

"The evidence in your hands shows the teeth of your lie," he said. "This is my Unfinished Business. I betrayed the men I loved, the men I fought alongside, the men who died. The men who gave their last drop of blood for a cause they believed in—and for me. And now that they are gone, there is no way to make amends."

The smoky outline of Mugwort went entirely white, then disappeared.

Alice closed the lid of the wooden box and climbed the stairs with the gold in her arms. She felt certain that eyes were upon her. As she stepped outside to go home, a sudden gust of wind blew through the drafty old House and shoved the door against her. There was no mistaking the feeling. She was being pushed out.

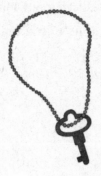

Chapter 14

"Do you think there's something going on at the house next door?" asked Alice's mother, staring out the window. As the days grew shorter, the shadow of the house grew longer, literally reaching into their living room in the fading afternoon light.

"The one that's condemned?" asked her husband. "I wouldn't think so."

"Is Alice home yet?"

"I'm right here," said Alice, who was standing at the end of the hall. She had just successfully slipped in through the front door, tiptoed down to the basement, and hidden the wooden box filled with gold doubloons. It fit neatly behind the small mountain of boxes that had yet to be unpacked from their latest move.

"Oh, Alice! When did you get home?" Professor Cannoli stretched out her long arms and scooped Alice into a hug. Alice could smell her mother's familiar aroma: the softness of her lavender soap mixed with the tangy scent of her dandruff shampoo. It would have been entirely lovely, except that Alice's nose was pressed into her mother's bony sternum. When her mother let go, Alice had to rub the end of her nose vigorously several times before everything settled back into its proper place.

"We were just talking about the house next door," said Alice's father, comfortably draping an arm over Alice's shoulder and kissing the top of her head.

"Why?" asked Alice cautiously.

"I've never been accused of being whimsical . . ." said Professor Cannoli.

"*That* is true," said her father.

"But lately I feel as though that house is *looking* at us. Isn't that ridiculous? The other day . . ." Alice's mother pushed her short black hair behind her ears, then shook her head so it all fell forward again. "It's too silly to say."

"What?" asked her husband. Mr. Potchnik never thought his wife was silly, even though she owned her own podium and delivered lectures in her own living room.

Alice's mother looked out the window. "I actually found myself *talking* to that house."

"I talk to houses all the time," said Alice's father.

"Yes, but you're a romantic, darling. And I most certainly am not."

"Again. Indisputable."

"The strangest part was, I felt like the house was *talking back* to me. Not with words. I can't describe it."

Alice crept up beside her mother, hardly able to breathe, and slipped her head under her mother's arm. "What do you think it was saying?" asked Alice in a whisper.

Alice's mother murmured, "Not 'saying.' Just a feeling. Something like . . . not to worry. Everything would be all right. And then . . ." She shook her head again, and for the first time in Alice's life, Alice saw her mother blush.

"What, Mom?" Alice held her breath, waiting to hear what the House had said.

"I *felt* like it said, *Thank you.* As if I had given it something of great value." She reached out for her husband's hand. "Absurd, isn't it?" She gave Alice another fierce, faint-inducing hug, then hurried to the kitchen to set the teakettle on the stove and hide the tears that were suddenly swimming in her eyes.

When her mother returned, she looked very much like her usual self, which emboldened Alice to pose the question she'd been wanting to ask: "Mom, where are my books from when I was little?"

"Packed away in one of the boxes in the basement," answered her mother, pouring the hot water into the teapot and dropping in three sachets of lapsang souchong tea. "I still can't muster the spirit to unpack in this house of disaster." She popped a tea cozy on top of the teapot. "Why do you need your old books?"

"Research," said Alice, and Alice's mother asked no more questions out of respect for the scholarly process.

Alice knocked on Professor Sosa's door at precisely ten o'clock, the moment when his office hours began. He cheerfully invited her in and pointed to the package that sat on his neat and orderly desk. "I didn't open it," he said. "I waited for you. Go ahead."

Alice snatched up the large, flat envelope with the word OVERNIGHT stamped across it and began to open it. The punch cards slipped out first, all neatly stacked and held together inside a protective plastic pouch that looked very official, as if it might have held important police evidence. Next, she pulled out a strange-looking stack of paper folded accordion-style. The paper had green and white stripes running across its width, and perforated edges, like pictures Alice had seen of old-fashioned rolls of film. There were faint words printed in monospace type across each page.

Professor Sosa leaned forward eagerly. "What is it? Mathematical calculations? Data for a science experiment? An engineering problem solved?"

"They're poems," said Alice. She opened the first accordion fold and placed the page on Professor Sosa's desk so they could read it together.

Sonnet for a Name I Love
(for Jenny)

The first time that I heard your lovely name,
I thought my heart would neatly break in two,
My eyes go blind, my ears go deaf, in vain,
For ne'er a boy like me, be liked by you.
Your laugh, your quiet eyes, and most of all
Intelligence that puts the rest of us
To shame. Of course, it is for her *I fall,*
Too smart to think that fate is, *or one plus*
This one could equal two. To you, I am
The quiet boy who never says a word,
Quiet fool, as speechless as a lamb,
Perhaps not there, he's seen but never heard.
    But when alone, so quiet, I whisper:
    Your lovely name, my own, my Jennifer.

Professor Sosa whistled. "Hoo! It's good. A bit over the top, I suppose. But it sounds like young love to me! Why were the poems hidden in code?"

"A secret love," said Alice. She turned a few more pages. Every poem was dedicated to Jenny. "Thank you so much for helping me, Professor Sosa."

Alice carefully placed the pages and the punch cards back in the envelope. She folded the top of the envelope over so the contents would be safe. "You know what I think?" she said. "I think love should never be a secret. It wasn't built for that."

"I tend to agree with you, Alice."

"Ivy!" said Alice, upon entering the House. "I need to talk to you!" Alice had learned that this type of "calling a spirit" didn't work. The ghosts were often out wandering or gathering energy by resting in the walls or just indifferent to her pleas. (It turned out that ghosts were much more like cats than dogs: they came when they wanted to, not when they were called.)

But this time, Ivy appeared, swirling out of the ceiling. She looked harried and disarranged, as if she'd been engaged in battle. "Thank goodness," she said. "I need a break!"

"A break from what?" asked Alice, but her words were drowned out by a smashing sound overhead. Ivy floated nervously to the ceiling and then back down again.

"Oh, dear, this is not a good day," Ivy fretted. "Not a good day at all." Her hair, usually curled neatly about her face, had turned into a tangle of vaporous tendrils that clutched and grasped at each other in the same way that Ivy was clutching and grasping her own misty hands.

There was another crash from above, followed by a scream and then a long wail, and someone began to pound on the attic floor. "One of the worst," said Ivy, pressing her ghostly hands to her ears. Her outline was ragged; she seemed to struggle to keep herself together.

"Ivy," said Alice, "*who* is up there?"

"Not allowed. Not allowed," said Ivy. "Some things are never spoken of." She was rising to the ceiling and falling again, as if she couldn't contain her nervous energy, all the while holding her hands over her ears.

"Well, I know this," said Alice. "It's not one of the Past Due, because they can't move things. And whatever's up there has the strength of ten elephants."

"It *is* a Past Due," said Ivy. "But it's so much worse. So, so much worse." Ivy suddenly swooped close and hovered alongside Alice's head. Alice could feel a cool dampness enter her ear canal and shoot down her spine, making her shiver. "It can do things. Things that no spirit should be able to do."

The House began to rumble. Ivy flew straight to the ceiling and then dropped so fast, she became a pool of agitated light on the floor.

"Tell me!" said Alice firmly.

"Never spoken of! Never spoken of!"

The House shook under Alice's feet. A warning. Perhaps it was best to leave this question unanswered, for now. *Patience,* her mother always said, *is not only a virtue, but a winning strategy.*

"Ivy," said Alice, speaking in a soothing voice, "I brought something to show you. Something very special. But you need to sit down on the sofa with me. You need to calm down."

Bit by bit, Ivy reconstituted herself from the puddle on the floor. When she was whole, she settled on the sofa next to Alice.

"What is it?" she asked, staring intently at the canvas tote bag by Alice's side. Her child's curiosity was getting the better of her. The sounds from upstairs had quieted. The House was still.

Alice reached into the canvas bag that held Danny's poems and pulled out a children's picture book.

"Oh! You found it!" said Ivy. "Where was it? Where did I hide it?"

"Ivy, this isn't your book. It's mine. I had the same book when *I* was a kid."

"Really?" said Ivy in disbelief. "That must be a one-in-a-million coincidence."

"Not really," said Alice. "It's a very famous book."

"No, it isn't! When I checked it out of the library, no one had even heard of it. Did I tell you I was the very first person to read it?"

"You did," said Alice.

"Did I tell you about the pajamas?"

"You did," said Alice.

"Did I tell you that I only got to read it one time before I died?"

Alice sucked in her breath. Ghosts sure had a way of saying things. "No. You didn't mention that."

"Will you read it to me now?" asked Ivy, and in her own way she curled up on Alice's lap and settled in for a story.

Alice opened the book to the first page: "In the great green room there was a telephone and a red balloon and a picture of—the cow jumping over the moon . . ."

When Alice finished reading the book, Ivy said, "I didn't remember all that. I thought it was just a book about a rabbit with terrific pajamas. But it's about time. And how time passes. And in the end, we have to say goodbye to everything we love, until we become nothing more than our essence."

"Yes," said Alice. "You know, I read this book about a hundred times when I was little, and I never thought about all that. But you're right."

"It isn't my book, though, is it?" asked Ivy. "This isn't the copy I checked out of the library." Ivy floated a few feet above Alice's lap.

"No," said Alice.

"So you can't return it to the library and get me Settled?"

"No, Ivy. It isn't a library book. We need to find *your* copy of the book. But now we know what we're looking for! That's got to help. Think, Ivy. Think really hard. Do you have any memory of where you hid it?"

"I was going on a trip," said Ivy slowly. "I was very excited. I packed my own valise. I wouldn't let anyone else carry it. It was all mine, and I was in charge of it."

Alice looked down at the small suitcase that Ivy carried, that she always carried, clutched tightly in her hand. "Ivy," she said slowly, "do you think . . . the book is in there?"

"Maybe!" said Ivy, quickly settling the suitcase on her lap. She tugged on a vaporous chain that hung around her neck, and from deep underneath the frilly collar of her dress appeared a tiny key no bigger than a baby grasshopper. Ivy turned the key in the lock, and a clasp sprang open.

Ivy lifted the lid of the valise.

Alice and Ivy peered inside.

There were three things in the suitcase: a toy spyglass, a pretend camera, and a plain notebook. All of them were made of nothing more than wispy vapor.

"I wanted to see *everything*. And I wanted to take pictures of *everything*. And I wanted to write it all down so I would never forget. I was so excited. I was going on a trip," said Ivy mournfully.

Alice could hardly swallow her own disappointment. "It was a good try," she managed to say. But then she had a thought. "Wait! Ivy, think of this. If you *had* packed the book in your valise, it would be vapor now, and you could never return it to the library. This way, there's still a chance we might find it in the living human world."

"That's true!" said Ivy, sounding slightly more hopeful.

"We'll try again tomorrow. I know we're going to find your library book, Ivy. But right now, we need to take Danny to see Professor Gurkenstein. Will you help me find him?"

Chapter 15

The index card on the door was gone, leaving nothing behind but a torn triangle of masking tape. The door was unlocked and ajar. The books, papers, and laptop were gone. Nothing remained but the abandoned plant on the desk, looking sicklier than ever.

Alice left the empty office and walked down the underground hallway, knocking on each door until she got a response. "Excuse me," she said to the man sitting behind a desk, grading papers. "Where is Professor Gurkenstein?"

The man looked up from his work. "Weird," he said. "Did it just get ten degrees colder in here?"

Alice didn't have time for his discomfort around ghosts.

"Do you know where she is?"

"Somewhere between here and the University of Minnesota. She was offered a permanent position there, so she took it."

"She's gone?" said Alice. "I don't have enough money to get to Minnesota!"

"I'm sorry," said the man, reaching for his sweater. "Is there a window open in the hallway? Would you mind closing the door on your way out?"

Alice walked slowly up the stairs to the lobby of the Modern Culture and Media building. She sat down on the first step. Leaning her head against the wall, she closed her eyes and whispered, "I'm so sorry, Danny. I thought I could do it. I thought I could get you Settled. I'm so sorry."

"Excuse me? Are you lost?"

Alice opened her eyes.

And there was Professor Gurkenstein, holding the handle of a very large, overstuffed suitcase on wheels.

"You're here," said Alice, stumbling to her feet. She felt a cool mist pass through her chest, and she knew that Danny had stepped closer to the love of his life.

"Oh, it's you!" said Professor Gurkenstein, showing her crooked tooth in her lovely smile. "I'm sorry, I don't remember your name."

"Alice."

"Right. Alice. You know, I actually attended one of your mother's lectures, out of curiosity. And everyone was right:

She *is* the best lecturer I've ever seen. She truly has a gift."

"Are you going to Minnesota?" asked Alice. "The man said . . ." Alice pointed down the stairs.

"Yes, I am. I have a cab waiting outside to take me to the airport. I just . . ." Professor Gurkenstein looked embarrassed and a little confused. "I came back . . . for the plant. I don't know why, really. But I was on my way to the airport, and I had this overwhelming feeling that I couldn't . . . just . . . *leave* it. They're not going to let me take it on the plane. I don't know why I came back for it." She threw both hands up in the air.

"You have to read some poems first," said Alice. "Before you leave."

"I'm afraid I can't. The taxi is waiting."

"You stay here and read these. I'll go to your office and get the plant. Think of how much time it will save you! You won't have to go down the stairs with that big suitcase. I'll be fast. You read." She stuffed the accordion paper into Professor Gurkenstein's hands and disappeared down the stairs.

When Alice arrived at the empty office, she scooped up the plant, but then stopped. It would take some time for Professor Gurkenstein to read enough of the poems. Alice sat down in the empty chair and counted to three hundred and fifty. Then she walked slowly down the hall and up the stairs. The taxi fare was going to be enormous.

When she got to the top of the stairs, Professor Gurkenstein was sitting on the floor, her hand on her heart. The poems rested in her lap, and her long silver braid hung over her shoulder and fell across the pages. Alice placed the dead plant beside her on the floor.

"I'm speechless," said Professor Gurkenstein.

Alice paused, and then pointed out, "Not really. You just said the words 'I'm speechless,' so that means, you know, that you're *not* actually speechless." She couldn't help herself; it was the Cannoli in her.

Professor Gurkenstein stared at her. "You're a very precise little girl," she finally said. "Where did you find these poems?"

"That's kind of a long story," said Alice, "and you have a plane to catch. But do you believe me now? Charlie loved you. He really, *really* loved you." It was all she could do to keep from saying, *And he still does.*

"I believe you." She shook her head back and forth, her hand still on her heart. "And I loved him. I wish there was some way I could make him know that."

There was a brightness, as if the shifting of the sun had suddenly caused a blinding glare on the windshield of a car. Alice squinted, and when she did, she saw Danny, but not as she had always seen him. In this split second of incandescence, he looked like a fully alive human being, solid and with every detail sharply defined. He was entirely there, and the light behind him caused him to shine like a supernova.

Alice reached out a hand. "Oh! Goodbye!" But Danny was already gone. He had advanced. He was now one of the Settled Ones.

"Yes, you're right," said Professor Gurkenstein, picking up the plant and standing. "I do need to be going. May I keep these?" she asked, holding out the poems.

Alice nodded. "They're yours."

"You look like you're going to cry," said Professor Gurkenstein, concerned.

"I'm fine," said Alice. "Really!"

But for the first time, she knew what it felt like to lose a friend.

In Memory of
Capt NATHANIEL
FINCH
1746 – 1799
He fought with honor
at the Battles of
Saratoga & Brandywine

Chapter 16

It would be kind to say that in the end both Ivy and Mugwort missed Danny and his weeping once he was gone, but this was not true. They were thrilled to have him out of the walls.

"Peace and quiet!" crowed Ivy, flying through the chandelier again and again as she played the game of refraction and reorganization. She zoomed past Alice, who was polishing a flea-market mirror she had restored.

"But don't you miss him at all?" Alice had been thinking a great deal about Danny's departure. She missed the way he puddled and rained, the look in his eyes when he spoke of Jenny, and the brave way he always showed exactly what he was feeling. She was surprised at how much it *hurt* to miss someone. Sometimes she felt the ache of missing him in her heart, and sometimes in the space behind her eyes, and sometimes in her teeth. "You *must* miss him a little," said Alice.

"No!" shouted Ivy, and Mugwort nodded. He was standing by the empty fireplace, staring into it as if a fire blazed within. Since the discovery of his betrayal, he had grown morose and withdrawn, sinking into a deep, dark place of recrimination and regret. Mugwort was very hard on his living self.

"Besides, Danny's Settled now," said Ivy. "It would be awfully selfish of us to wish him back."

"I suppose," said Alice, recognizing again that she still experienced time as a human, not as spirits did. Ivy and Mugwort lived in the past, the present, and the future all at once, which was the same as living outside of time altogether. Alice couldn't quite get the hang of it. "I miss him, though."

"Oh, look!" said Ivy. "It's that truck you love so much, Alice. The one that leaves little bits of paper for you." Ivy had long ago forgotten the purpose of daily mail delivery.

"The mail truck?" asked Alice, leaping to her feet. "I'll be right back."

She sprinted next door and scooped a pile of letters and magazines out of the crooked, rusted mailbox that sat on the porch of the Cannoli-Potchnik house. The mailbox had fallen off years ago, but Professor Cannoli wouldn't allow Mr. Potchnik to hang it again. "Victory shall be ours!" said Professor Cannoli whenever her husband asked about rewiring a lighting fixture or caulking the tub.

"Nothing, nothing, nothing," muttered Alice, flipping through the mail. "Oh." There it was! The letter she'd been waiting for!

She returned next door and found Mugwort in the same spot she had left him. "Mugwort, do you know these names?" She began to read from the letter. "Private Jacob Stout. Private Daniel Carson. First Lieutenant Ebenezer Howcroft. Corporal Samuel Townsend. Second Lieutenant Phineas Drummond. Private George Alford. Private John Bingler. Sergeant Charles Millings. Private Benjamin Stokes."

Mugwort's face erased itself, then fell back into its regular features. He seemed perplexed and agitated. "I do. But I don't know how." The outline of his teeth wobbled and his earlobes drooped down to his shoulders.

"They're the men who fought with you in your company in the Ninth Regiment. I sent a letter to a special Revolutionary War society, asking if they had the muster roll for your regiment, and they did! These are the men in your company." Alice paused. Mugwort stood as if frozen in place, and yet the outline of his body vibrated with a frightening intensity. Alice worried he would break apart. To soothe him, she murmured, "They fought and won at the Battle of Saratoga. They lost with honor at the Battle of Brandywine."

"My men," said Mugwort quietly. "My men."

"Yes. The men you fought beside." Alice picked up her bag. "Now that I have their names, I have more research to do. But

I'll be back. Try not to be sad while I'm gone." She turned to Ivy and said, "And don't worry. This may take some time." She hurried to the back door and left.

Mugwort stayed rooted to his spot. Ivy continued to float by the window, watching the round globe of the sun rise and fall, and rise and fall, and rise and fall again.

"I'm back!" shouted Alice, banging the back door behind her. "Were you worried?" She stopped short when she entered the parlor. "You're both right where I left you!"

"What's strange about that?" asked Ivy.

"Jeepers! I've been gone for three days!" said Alice.

"Well, you can't expect us to keep track of *that*," said Ivy. "One time Mugwort sat on the sofa and read the newspaper for a year. At least I think it was a year. All the seasons went by before he finished."

"Unbelievable," murmured Alice.

"Did you find anything good? With your research?" asked Ivy.

"Great. *Fantastic*, actually." Alice turned to Mugwort, who was still standing by the fireplace. "I took the names from that letter. The names of the men in your company in the Ninth Regiment. And I visited the oldest cemetery here in town. There are a lot of Revolutionary War graves there. A *lot*. It took some time. And effort!" Alice looked down at her hands, which were scraped, blistered, and bruised. "But I found the graves of *seven* of the men in your company."

"Seven graves? My men—they're dead, then?" asked Mugwort.

"Yes," said Alice pointedly. It was strange to her that she needed to remind Mugwort that the men he had fought with two hundred and fifty years ago—even the ones who had survived the war—were no longer alive.

"All of them?" asked Mugwort cautiously.

"Yes, all of them," said Alice, feeling a bit impatient. "I found their graves, though. I had to hunt all over the cemetery, and pull away brambles, and scrape off moss. Some of the headstones had broken in two. That's why it took so long. But I found the graves of seven of them." She paused, as if she wasn't sure she should go on. "I even found your grave, Mugwort."

"Mine?" he asked, as if surprised that he was dead too.

"Yes," said Alice. "It's a very beautiful headstone with an angel's face and wings carved into it. It's simple and dignified, not showy at all. And it sits right under a sturdy oak tree. I'm going to go back next time and plant some mugwort in front of it."

"I've never seen my grave," said Mugwort. He turned away from Alice.

"I think I figured something out," said Alice. "How to make amends. How to finish your Unfinished Business of the Heart."

Ivy swooped in closer, suddenly interested. Even Mugwort cocked his head to listen better, though he didn't turn to face her.

"There's a society that takes care of the graves of soldiers in the cemetery. They keep the graves neat and leave flowers and put out those little American flags on Memorial Day. They even offer historical tours of the graves. But they're almost out of money. You could give them some of your gold. Your men would be taken care of and remembered forever."

Ivy circled around to face Mugwort. "It's almost like they would still be alive," she said.

Mugwort didn't move.

"But there would still be lots of gold coins left, and I don't think you should keep any of them," said Alice. "So, I have another idea. I thought you could donate the rest to the local Soldiers' Home. Because the soldiers there *are* still living, and they sure do need help."

Mugwort continued to stand with his back to Alice. "Money?" he asked. "Do you think I can buy my way out of my Unfinished Business?"

"Money is very important to living humans," said Ivy, "though I can't even remember what it's for."

"I don't know for sure that it'll work," said Alice, "but it's worth a try. You *made* money when you were in the war—that was your betrayal. It seems to me that if you give that money back to the soldiers you harmed and to other soldiers too, well, that's a pretty good way to make amends."

"But the gold means nothing to me," said Mugwort. "I'm not truly giving up anything by giving it away."

"It's the best you've got," said Alice quietly. "I know how

much you *wish* you could undo the things you did when you were alive. Maybe that wish—with a few Spanish coins thrown in—will do the trick."

Mugwort sighed. "Try if you must. I hold out no hope." He turned to face Alice. "Whether it works or not, I owe you a great debt of gratitude. Your efforts are valiant, and your motives are pure. You would have been the finest of soldiers, Alice." He bowed curtly and disappeared into the wall.

There was an unfamiliar sight in the driveway of the Cannoli-Potchnik house: a car. Neither Professor Cannoli nor Mr. Potchnik owned one. They both considered cars to be unnecessary, messy, expensive headaches. Of course, the fact that neither one of them knew how to drive just made their opinions more unyielding.

Alice walked in through the front door. When she entered, her mother greeted her with an enormously wide and somewhat ghoulish grin. It made Alice gasp to see so many of her mother's teeth all at once.

"Alice, my darling," said Professor Cannoli, holding out a hand for her daughter to take. "Dean Sheridan has come for tea."

Dean Sheridan was the dean of faculty, which meant her job was to keep all the professors *happy* and to keep all the professors *in line*. Sometimes these two missions were in direct conflict.

One of the things Alice liked best about Dean Sheridan

was that her shoes always matched her dress. Exactly. When Dean Sheridan bought a new dress, she bought a new pair of white shoes and had them hand-dyed to be the exact color of the dress. Before meeting Dean Sheridan, Alice hadn't known that you could dye shoes. So that was something interesting.

The fact that Dean Sheridan's shoes always matched her dress was precisely the thing that Professor Cannoli found most suspect about Dean Sheridan.

"Alice, I haven't seen you since the campus spelling bee last spring," said Dean Sheridan. "To this day, it's my pride and my shame that our best team of college students was defeated by a ten-year-old. What was the final word again?"

"*Auftaktigkeit*," said Alice, shaking Dean Sheridan's hand, as she'd been taught to do, "the principle in music where all musical phrases begin on an upbeat. But it wasn't just me. We were a team." The Cannoli-Potchnik spelling team was feared throughout the county, and ever since that particular win, they'd been banned from participating in campus contests.

"Speaking of team efforts," said Professor Cannoli, "I was just showing Dean Sheridan around the house. It's hard to believe it's been a whole month since we first moved in."

A whole month? To Alice it felt like she'd known Ivy and Mugwort for *years*. Time. It was a slippery fish.

"Yes," said Dean Sheridan, laughing in a self-conscious way. "I have to admit, I came by filled with curiosity to see what amazing improvements you've made. You always trans-form the houses you live in."

"It's true," said Professor Cannoli, smiling the iron-jawed grin that alarmed Alice. "But as I said before, we like this house *just the way it is*. Every imperfection feels like a gift. Every flaw is filled with beauty. We don't plan on changing a single thing."

Alice's father came in carrying a tray filled with a teapot, teacups, and cookies. "I'm afraid they're from the store," he apologized to Dean Sheridan. "Normally I bake, but the oven doesn't work. And I think there's a birds' nest in the vent, anyway."

"Alice," said Dean Sheridan, "how do *you* like living in this house?" She looked at Alice as if she expected a certain kind of answer. Perhaps one that would put her parents in an uncomfortable spot.

Alice shrugged. "I don't care. As long as we stay put, I'm happy." She picked up a shortbread cookie and snapped it in two. "Nice shoes, Dean Sheridan!" Then she put half the cookie in her mouth, which even she knew was outside the bounds of both politeness *and* safety.

"Thank you, Alice." Dean Sheridan's shoes were a robin's egg blue, which matched her dress, just barely visible under the fall coat she had kept on during her visit to the drafty house. "I must be off," she said, affecting disappointment. "No tea for the wicked, as they say." She stood and adjusted the collar of her coat. "At least you'll have more afternoon light after the demolition."

"Demolition?" asked Professor Cannoli.

"Yes, the house next door," said Dean Sheridan. "I pushed the board to set a date."

"What?" shouted Alice, spitting cookie out of her mouth.

"Past due, if you ask me," said Dean Sheridan.

Alice spluttered, coughing up more cookie crumbs.

"It's hard to find money to build a new college building, but harder still to find the money to tear one down," said Dean Sheridan, pulling her gloves out of her coat pocket. "That house has been condemned for twenty years. We had to fight the Historic Preservation Society *and* the local neighborhood association *and* the town itself, but everybody has finally given up. The demolition work begins on Monday. We're very much hoping that a wrecking ball will do the job. It's prohibitively expensive to use explosives."

Alice gasped, inhaling cookie bits, which brought on a fearsome coughing attack.

"That's a shame," said Mr. Potchnik, whacking his daughter on the back. "From the outside, the house is a real beauty." He shook his head, genuinely sad. "Too bad there wasn't anyone around to take care of it. Alice, are you all right?" Alice waved to signal that she was fine, but continued sputtering and gasping.

"Well, we're a college," said Dean Sheridan, peering out the window at the lowering clouds and retrieving her compact umbrella from her bag, "not a restoration club."

"I'll miss it," said Professor Cannoli, a comment so sentimental that it surprised everyone in the room, most of all her.

"Alice, darling? Are you choking?"

Her father continued with the whacking and her mother prepared to lift her upside down and shake her by the ankles. Suddenly, a soggy hunk of cookie shot out of her mouth and landed on the toe of Dean Sheridan's shoe. "Monday?" Alice gasped. "But today is Thursday. Do you mean they're taking down the house in just four days?"

Dean Sheridan shook her toe, but the cookie stuck. She was not pleased. "Yes. The crew is scheduled to arrive at seven o'clock on Monday morning. They like to get an early start. I'm told it goes very quickly. The demolition part. The cleanup takes longer, even with the bulldozers." She turned to Alice's parents. "Thank you for the visit. I always enjoy spending time with your entertaining family. And I'm particularly pleased that the college has provided you with a house that is *completely* to your satisfaction. Many years of happiness!" And she disappeared under the canopy of her umbrella.

Chapter 17

"*What* never happens?" Alice asked for the third time.

Ivy was being her usual stubborn self, but even more so. "*It* never happens! Houses don't fall down. And I can tell you *this* house isn't going to collapse. It was built to last!"

"But it's *condemned*," said Alice. It was the morning after Dean Sheridan's visit. Alice had woken early, before the sun was up, and delivered two packages: one to the doorstep of the founder of the Friends of the Mount Hope Cemetery and the other to the doorstep of the Soldiers' Home. Each anonymous package contained some of the gold coins with specific instructions on how the money was to be used.

Alice couldn't find the courage to tell Ivy that the House

was going to be torn down in *three* days, and she couldn't bear to think that the House was listening to her. So she had been asking Ivy a *what-if* question: *What if* a house like this collapses when there are still Past Due spirits inside?

"Oh, fiddle faddle," said Ivy, swinging her valise in a care-free way. "That sign has been on the door *forever*. Nothing changes."

"Things do change, Ivy! They change a lot. Time goes by, you just don't know it. You didn't know how to tell time when you were alive, and you definitely don't know how to tell time now that you're dead!"

"It isn't kind to point out someone's shortcomings. I think I'm very angry at you!" said Ivy tartly, but she floated up to the ceiling and sailed back down in a lazy corkscrew, so Alice didn't think she was really angry at all. And then Alice realized that perhaps Ivy was struggling with her own feelings about change. It was easy to forget that Ivy was a child, in part because she talked like a grownup and in part because she was more than seventy years old. But perhaps Ivy was frightened. She was working so very hard *not* to answer Alice's question.

Alice sat on the couch and let Ivy float to the ceiling and corkscrew down several more times. Then she said, "I know the House will stand forever. It has a stone foundation and is set deep in the ground. It was built to outlast the ages, and it will. But what if a house—a *different* house—was torn down and there were still spirits inside, waiting to complete their Unfinished Business of the Heart? What would become of *them*?"

Ivy landed gently on the sofa cushion next to Alice. "It is the worst fate of all. Even worse than being a Forever Forgotten, they say. When the house falls, when the last stone is tumbled and the final wall is broken to pieces, the essence of any spirit living in the house is shattered into tiny particles that are cast throughout the universe. The particles spend the rest of eternity trying to find each other, trying to make their essence whole. But a spirit with Unfinished Business that loses its last home can never be reconstituted. There's no way to find every last particle. And so the spirit spends all of eternity shattered."

Alice tried to imagine such a thing. To always feel that a part of you was missing. To know that you could never come home.

"But it never happens," said Ivy with assurance. "Humans almost never die in their own homes these days. They're always in hospitals or cars or at a baseball game. And the old houses, like this one, are built to last. Plus, they're protected by all kinds of preservation societies. Who would tear down a beautiful old house like this?"

Alice felt a thrum in the air and knew that the House had been listening. She couldn't tell if it was a hum of pleasure at Ivy's compliment or a shiver of dread as the House sensed the urgency in Alice's voice.

"Ivy," she said. "We are going to find your library book *today*."

"We are?" asked Ivy, wide-eyed. "How exciting! I'm going

on a trip! I can take the book with me."

"It must be in the House somewhere. I'm going to make a systematic search of every room." She pulled her builder's notebook out of her canvas bag and made a quick diagram of the first floor. She would have to map out the second floor when she got there, since she'd never set foot upstairs. The House had seen to that.

Alice started in the back parlor. It was a relatively easy room to search because it had so little in it, but Alice was certain to tap on the wooden panels of the walls in case there was a secret cupboard and to press on every floorboard on the chance that one might be loose and reveal a hiding place below.

The kitchen was harder. There were many cupboards and pantries, high shelves and closets. Alice spent an hour in that room alone. Ivy flitted about her head or coiled herself around Alice's body, she was so excited. That much mingling with Ivy's essence left Alice feeling out of sorts. It also left her slightly damp and definitely chilled.

When Alice finished searching downstairs, she was tired, discouraged, and dirty. She'd spent so much time fixing the front parlor that she'd forgotten the condition of the rest of the House. Rotted floorboards, broken windows, mouse droppings, and discarded trash were in every room. The rediscovery of the ruin felt like a defeat. What did it matter if she'd made the front parlor look like new? It was a single room within a sinking wreck.

And still she had not found Ivy's book.

Alice looked at Ivy, who was floating on her back in the foyer, her valise resting comfortably on her stomach. "What do you think, Ivy? Should we check the basement or upstairs?"

"Oh, not the basement," said Ivy. "I never liked the basement. It scared me! I played in the attic every chance I got . . ."

"The attic?" asked Alice. "You spent a lot of time in the attic?"

"Oh, yes!" said Ivy. "It was filled with treasures and surprises, and there were so many places to hide. I loved to hide."

"The attic, Ivy! The book is in the attic!"

Alice put her foot on the first step of the staircase, but Ivy flew in front of her and said, "You mustn't go upstairs! *You mustn't!*"

"Because of all the noises?" asked Alice. "Because"—what had been the seed of an idea germinating in her brain suddenly bloomed into a fully formed flower—"there's a Captive up there?"

"You don't understand," shrieked Ivy. "It isn't like the rest of us!"

"In my experience," said Alice, and here she was quoting her mother, because Alice herself had no experience whatsoever in this area, "the more fuss a person makes, the less danger they are." She quoted her mother airily: "It's all *Sturm und Drang.*" When her mother said these words, you could believe them. Alice wasn't so sure, and she trembled at the thought of going up to the attic. She was, however, resolved.

"The House will never allow it!" declared Ivy. "And neither

will I!" Ivy placed herself between Alice and the staircase.

Alice's heart melted a little. This was the sweetest thing she'd ever seen Ivy do. But also the silliest.

"Oh, Ivy," said Alice. "You can't block my way. You're only . . . dampness. And besides, I'm utterly determined."

Ivy bobbed resolutely in front of the staircase. *You will not pass.* She said it with such fortitude that Alice almost believed her. Perhaps there was some hidden power in Ivy that Alice wasn't aware of? Did she have a trick up her vaporous sleeve?

Alice clenched both hands into fists and crossed her arms at the wrists over her chest, creating a shield in front of her body as if she were going to war. "Ivy, you've never seen the famous Cannoli-Potchnik Oath, so prepare yourself." She stretched herself to her full height. "I take this solemn Cannoli-Potchnik Oath: I am going to find that book and I am going to get you Settled before Monday, if it's the last thing I do! And no house, not even this one, is going to stop me!" She then extended her fists, still crossed, in front of her, as if leading a charge.

"Wait!"

Alice was startled to hear Mugwort's voice. She turned, her arms still extended. "Mugwort!" she said. "You look different!" His outline was more solid than usual, and there was just a hint of color in his shape. His uniform was blue and the epaulet on his right shoulder was gold, while the sash across his waist was red. The colors were faint, but they were there. The brass on the polished hilt of his sword glinted ever so slightly.

"I feel different," he said. "Very different. I can *feel* the ground underneath my feet. It's been many lifetimes since I could feel that."

"Oh, Mugwort," said Alice. "It's happening."

"But why like this?" asked Ivy, swirling busily around Mugwort. "You said when Danny went, it happened all at once."

Alice looked at her watch. It was almost nine o'clock in the morning. Perhaps the founder of the volunteer society had gone out, still in her slippers and bathrobe, to retrieve her morning newspaper and had found the package that Alice had left right beside her paper. But perhaps the package at the Soldiers' Home hadn't been found yet. "It's still early," said Alice.

"No. It's late," said Mugwort.

The room was flooded with a blinding light, as if the sun had just risen over the horizon. Alice shielded her eyes with her hands. For a brief instant she saw Mugwort, standing tall, his sword at his side, just as he had looked when he was alive. His medals shone brightly on his chest, and the gold braid epaulet on his shoulder shivered as he turned to look at her once more. Then he was gone.

There hadn't been time to say goodbye.

Chapter 18

Alice stood quietly at the foot of the stairs. The intense light had created a dim afterimage of Mugwort that seemed to float before Alice's eyes. It was almost like having him back in his ghostly form, but the ache in her heart told her that he was gone forever. Alice stared at the spot where Mugwort had stood until she heard a muffled sniffling and turned to see Ivy, her head bent over her knees as she crouched in midair.

"Oh, Ivy," said Alice, who wished that she could give the small child one of her mother's Cannoli hugs, fierce and protective and full of love. But it wasn't possible. Such an embrace would simply pass through the mist that was the last incarnation of Ivy.

Ivy gasped between her sobs. "We mustn't be . . . sad. He's . . . Settled now. It's just . . . that . . . he was my . . . oldest friend."

"I'm so sorry, Ivy," said Alice. "I'm sorry that you're sad!"

Ivy looked up, startled out of her crying. "I *am* sad. It's been so long since I felt anything like this. It's almost like being alive again." She pressed her lips together and wrinkled her six-year-old brow. "Being alive was hard," she finally said. "Too many feelings."

The clock in the parlor chimed nine times, reminding Alice that the day was passing. She looked at Ivy with renewed determination.

"I'm going to *find that book*," said Alice.

Ivy began to swarm around Alice's head like a fly on a hot day in July. "No! No! You mustn't go up to the attic. It's quiet now. If you go up—I don't know what will happen."

"Then let's find out," said Alice.

"I've just lost Mugwort," wailed Ivy. "I don't want to lose you, too!"

But Alice rushed up the stairs, half expecting the House to pull the entire staircase out from under her. When the structure held, Alice wondered if her mistake last time had been her caution and tentativeness. Maybe this was a situation that required a bold attack.

Alice reached the second-floor landing, then rushed down the hall to the door at the back of the house that led to the attic. In the old days, the attic would have been the servants' quarters. Fittingly, the door was plain and obscure, almost hidden around a corner. Ivy flitted around Alice's head, begging her to stop. Alice grasped the doorknob, then pulled her hand away.

The doorknob was *hot*—not as hot as a stovetop, but hot enough that it hurt to touch. Alice pulled the sleeve of her shirt down over her hand and grabbed the knob again. As she did, she heard the familiar rattle and then click of a door chain. Alice pushed, but the chain prevented the door from opening.

"Alice, you mustn't! The House doesn't want you to go up there!"

"Who said the House always gets what it wants?" shouted Alice. Ivy gasped so loudly that she dissolved. But Alice didn't think it was the House that was throwing up roadblocks. If the House hadn't wanted her to go to the attic, it would have destroyed the staircase—and Alice with it. Alice felt that a *different* presence was trying to keep her out, one that had many fewer tricks up its sleeve: a hot doorknob and a rusted door chain. Alice was not impressed.

Alice kicked at the door. The wood in the door jamb was badly rotted through. The chain broke from its moorings and the door flew open.

The stairs up to the attic were dim and narrow, and the treads on the steps were deeply scarred. When Alice put her foot on the first step, a tremendous wind, as hot as the desert, blew down the attic staircase, pushing her back into the hallway so forcefully that she fell down.

Alice stood up and shouted, "Sorry to disappoint you, but I'm coming up anyway."

She grabbed ahold of the splintery banister, tucked her chin to her chest, and leaned into the wind. Step by step, she pulled herself up the stairs. When she reached the top, the wind stopped abruptly. Alice looked up, expecting to see a rotted roof beam about to drop on her head or a vaporous fog ready to smother her.

But the attic was ordinary. There were some derelict pieces of furniture: a table that was missing one leg, two mismatched armchairs with their stuffing erupting from the cushions, several bookcases filled with dusty books, a floor lamp with a tasseled lampshade, a wool rug eaten through by moths. In one corner, a broom and dustpan leaned against the wall. Two brick chimneys rose like columns from the floor to the ceiling on each end of the room, but only one had a small garret fireplace, just large enough to hold a single piece of wood or a small heap of coal. The fireplace was swept clean; it had not seen a fire for many years.

The oddity of the attic, Alice noticed, was that it had a "lived-in" feeling. It was easy to imagine two old friends sitting companionably in those armchairs, sharing a pot of tea on that three-legged table, and reading books from the bookcase in the warm glow of the lamp. In fact, the furniture was arranged in just that way.

"Oh," whispered Ivy, who had reconstituted herself. "It's building up. It's growing stronger. We have to leave, *now.*"

"It's in the walls?" whispered Alice.

Ivy shook her head and pointed to one of the chimneys, which were rooted in the stone foundation of the basement and rose up through the roof. "It's like the House," whispered Ivy. "It gains strength from stone and brick."

"Why is it a Captive?"

"The worst thing of all: It betrayed someone it loved *while they both lived in the House.* And it died in this room. *Without making amends!* It must have been a terrible betrayal, because it can *move* things. I've never known an essence with that power."

An armchair suddenly flew up in the air and flipped itself over.

Ivy's outline began to tremble and break apart. "It's awake. The Fury is awake."

"The Fury? Why did the House name it that?" All the other spirits were named after things that grew in the garden.

Ivy shook her trembling head. "The House didn't name it. It named *itself*!" She flitted to the far corner of the attic.

A lamp knocked itself over, the glass bulb shattering on the floor. A bookcase toppled. As the books fell from the shelves Alice caught a glimpse of a familiar cover. She lunged for the book, but the heavy bookcase fell on top of it. A screaming filled Alice's ears, and she was lifted up as if by a tornado and thrown across the room. She would have smashed her head into the wall but for a counterwind that slowed her flight and gave her a chance to land on all fours.

"Thank you," whispered Alice, staggering to her feet. It made her feel safer, knowing that the House was present. But then again, the House was always present.

One of the books that had skittered halfway across the floor rose up in the air and came hurtling at her body. Alice skipped to one side, narrowly dodging the book. Another flew through the air, with just as much force, and Alice managed to evade that one, too. But the third book—the full volume of *Peter Pan*, complete with illustrations—hit her squarely on the side of her head and knocked her to the ground.

Flattened, Alice had trouble thinking straight. Should she get up or remain on the floor? The floor felt safe and soothing, but she knew there was danger if she stayed there. Something was advancing on her.

She pressed her hand to the sore spot on her head where the book had collided with her skull. When she looked at her fingers, she saw blood.

"Get up!'" whispered Ivy urgently. "Oh, please, Alice! Please, please! Get up and let's get out of here. The Fury's out of control."

Ivy's urging and the sight of her own blood cleared Alice's

brain. She knew she had to get up. She knew she had to get out. But not before she got the book she had glimpsed.

Alice pushed herself to her hands and knees and then stood up. As she moved to the overturned bookcase, she caught sight of the Fury in a corner of the attic. This spirit wasn't made of light, as Ivy was and Mugwort and Danny had been. Instead, it was the angry scribbling of a tormented mind, a tangled mess of charcoal-black lines that looked like a cyclone, twisting and churning. It was a temper tantrum, an explosive scrawling of chaos and rage.

The tornado rushed at Alice.

An unseen force pushed the Fury back into the corner. It shrieked and howled, regathering its strength, then threw itself at Alice.

Again something held it back, but the Fury had come closer. On its third assault, the Fury advanced to within a few feet of Alice before being pushed back to its corner, where it settled into a heaving mass of tangles.

Alice feared that the strength of the House was being sapped and that she had only a short amount of time to retrieve the book. What would happen to her if the Fury reached her and wrapped her up in the twisting core of its wrath?

Alice dashed to the bookcase. She tried to lift it, but it was too heavy. Ivy flew by her side to help. She even put down her precious valise to aid in the effort, but she was unable to exert any force on the heavy bookcase.

The Fury rushed at Alice, shrieking like the rusted brakes on a train going off its rails. Ivy flew up and threw herself at the Fury. The power of the impact scattered Ivy into a thousand pieces all over the attic.

"Ivy!" shouted Alice. The collision seemed to have damaged the Fury, too. Spirals spun out of its weakened center, and it was unable to advance.

Alice grabbed hold of the overturned bookcase and pulled up with all her strength, lifting the way her father had taught her to carry heavy pieces of lumber. But she could only get the bookcase to rise an inch or two. She dropped it back to the floor.

The Fury was in the far corner, spinning and twisting, gathering and consolidating its anger, like a hurricane at sea that funnels the energy of the ocean into its dark eye.

Alice once again grasped the edge of the bookcase and tried to lift. Suddenly, Ivy was at her side, reconstituted, but more wobbly than before. She tried to imitate Alice, wrapping her vaporous fingers around the wooden edge of the bookcase, but there was no way for her to grasp the heavy piece of furniture, let alone lift it.

Meanwhile, the Fury had grown to twice its original size. It now stretched from floor to ceiling, and Alice heard the buzzing of what sounded like thousands of hornets disturbed in their nest. The Fury was starting to inch closer to Alice and Ivy.

"We can't lift it ourselves," said Alice to Ivy. "We need a tool."

Ivy flew up to the ceiling, where the heavy chandelier hung above their heads, in order to get a better look. "I don't see any! I wish you had your bag with you!"

Alice had been thinking the same thing. But she was also thinking about her father's lessons on simple machines. If she could *wedge* one book under the bookcase and then wedge another book on top of the first book and then wedge one more book on top of that—maybe she could reach under to retrieve the precious book. She grabbed one of the books that had spilled free—a book with a thick spine—and shoved it into the space between the bookcase and the floor.

The Fury was upon her. Ivy flew away from the chandelier, which swung back and forth furiously, reacting to the angry swell of energy around it. Ivy darted in and out, trying to attack the Fury from all sides, but the Fury spun faster and faster, throwing Ivy off as quickly as she advanced.

When the Fury reached Alice, it rose up, compressing itself against the ceiling and hovering above Alice, who was holding on to the bookcase to keep from being thrown across the room. Alice looked up and saw that the Fury was preparing to smash down on her like a giant foot poised above a cockroach. She heard her mother's oft-told advice: *Timing is everything!*

She waited.

In the split second after the Fury began to descend, Alice pushed herself with all her strength and rolled out of the away. The Fury landed with its full force on the bookcase, splintering it to pieces. The heavy chandelier, which had been caught in the center of the Fury's deadly spiral, wrenched free of the hook that held it to the ceiling and crashed down.

The Fury imploded, collapsing in on itself until it was a dark puddle the size of a dinner plate. Alice stared at it. Was it over? Had they won?

The puddle began to expand, oozing its way to the far corner of the room. It was like a dark sludge filled with writhing worms. The scribbles were beginning to join, amassing their energy, which had been momentarily scattered.

Alice knew that the Fury would rise up, stronger than ever.

"Ivy!" shouted Alice. "Help me find the book!"

Alice scrambled to the heap of splintered wood that had been the bookcase and began scraping and clawing through the rubble of books.

"I see it!" squeaked Ivy, who was barely recognizable. Her outline had devolved into a loose collection of disjointed lines and curves. Her valise was entirely absent.

Alice pounced on the book with the familiar green cover and yellow letters. Out of the corner of her eye, she saw that the Fury was beginning to rise again, spiraling out of the puddle and marshaling all the broken bits of energy into a single long twisted strand of rage.

"Let's go!" shouted Alice, scrambling for the stairs that led down to the second floor. Ivy flew bravely at her shoulder as she descended. The door blew open ahead of them and, once they were through, it slammed shut with a bang. Alice could hear the Fury pounding against the door, but the door held fast, even though it wasn't locked. As Alice and Ivy hurried to the staircase that would take them to safety, Alice once again thought, *Thank you. Thank you, House.*

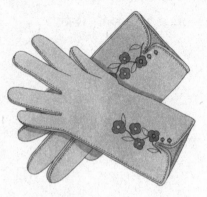

Chapter 19

A few drops of blood dribbled down the side of Alice's head, and she could see bruises appearing on her upper arm where the Fury had thrown her against the wall. She also had a crimson mark on her cheek and a tear on the left knee of her jeans.

Ivy was in much worse shape. She was nearly fragmented, and the only feature of hers that was clearly visible was her right eye. The rest of her body was nothing more than mist, and when she turned one way or the other, she left pieces of herself behind.

"It's the book, Ivy," said Alice, turning the pages. "A first edition, just like you said. And look, you were the only person to check it out of the library." Alice pointed to the brown and crumbling slip of paper glued onto the inside of the cover with lines printed across it. The one name written on the top of the checkout slip was Patience Hathaway.

"Patience!" said Ivy. "What a mistake of a name for *me*! I'd much rather be Ivy."

Alice found the name of the library stamped on the title page. "It's only five blocks from here," she said. "You stay here and rest in the walls, and I'll go return it."

"No," said Ivy, as stubborn as ever. "I'm going, too."

Alice walked slowly, in part because her knee hurt, but also because Ivy was limping beside her, not having the strength to materialize ahead, as ghosts usually do. The bottom half of her had unwound and trailed behind her like the tail of a comet. Of course, once they left the House, Ivy disappeared from Alice's sight entirely, but Alice knew she was there.

When they turned onto the walkway that led to the hundred-year-old library, Ivy reappeared. Her outline was faint, but Alice could see all her buttons and the bow on her dress and the valise she carried once more. Alice felt sure now that the House could communicate with other buildings through the bedrock underground. She imagined the House telling the old stone library of their approach and requesting that the library bestow a temporary blessing on them: the Blessing of the Library. It would make this part easier, being able to see Ivy.

"You were wonderful, Ivy," said Alice.

"Oh, I didn't do much."

"Are you kidding? You kept fighting the Fury, even after it

threw your essence all over the place. And *you* found the book."

"I did!" said Ivy, some of the old delight returning to her voice. "We make a pretty good team."

"Yeah," said Alice, slowing to a snail's pace as she approached the front door.

"Are you going to drop it through the slot?" asked Ivy.

Alice hesitated. If she did, the book might not make its way to the return desk for hours, maybe even a whole day. A whole day with Ivy. Her last day with Ivy.

"No," said Alice. "I'm going to take it inside and put it on the return desk." It was the safest thing to do.

There was already a pile of books waiting to be processed, and Alice placed the long-overdue book at the very bottom of the stack. Then she retreated to a corner of the lobby near the door and waited, keeping her eyes strictly on the librarian checking in books.

"Ivy," said Alice. "I want to tell you that—" Oh! How she wished she had her mother's gift of speech, the famous Cannoli rhetoric, of which it was said that it could make foolish men wise, wise men good, and good men weep. But Alice had not inherited her mother's talent at turning a phrase. Instead, she heard her father's voice, quietly full of love, that said, *Alice, my darling girl, speak from your heart. Leave nothing left unsaid.* Alice never wanted to have Unfinished Business of the Heart.

"I know," said Ivy quietly. "You're my best friend, too. I'm so glad the House brought you to us."

"The House brought me to you?"

"Well, almost. I think—I can't be sure—but I think the House was trying to bring you and your family to live in the House itself. It got you as close as the house next door, and then *you* came over to the House, all on your own."

Alice didn't know what to make of this news. It had never occurred to her that it had been anything more than a coincidence that the Cannoli-Potchnik family had, after all their many moves over the past ten years, ended up next door to the International House of Dereliction. But then, when she thought about their last ten addresses, she realized that her family *had* been steadily moving closer and closer to this last house.

Alice glanced at the return desk and saw that the librarian had already worked her way through half the books. She seemed to be an unusually efficient person.

"Ivy, I don't understand, why would the House—"

"Everyone wants things settled in the end, don't you think? A good ending? Sometimes I think that Danny and Mugwort and me—that we're the Unfinished Business of the *House*, but I don't really know about that. I suppose that doesn't make sense. A House is not the same as a spirit." She shook her ragged head. "There's a lot about the House I'll never understand, even though I've lived there my whole life and my whole death."

"Ivy. There's something I want to say to you." Alice looked again at the checkout desk. There were only three books remaining.

"I know, I know," said Ivy, who also seemed to sense the urgency of the moment, even without checking the progress of the librarian. "But I have one more thing I have to say to you. You have to promise me something."

The Potchnik in her would have said *Anything!* but the Cannoli in her would have asked *What?* Alice remained silent.

Ivy's wavering outline held itself firm. "Promise me you'll be kind to the Fury."

"What? *No!*" said Alice. "Look what it did to you!"

"I'm fine. I just need to reconstitute. But the Fury's in agony. Something unbearable happened. You have a big heart, Alice. Show kindness. Forgive—for whatever it did when it was a faulted and frail living human."

The librarian had picked up Ivy's overdue book. Alice felt her breath catch in her lungs. The librarian stared at the book, looking at the front and then the back, and then flipping to the page with the checkout slip. She called over another librarian, and then two more quickly joined them. Alice could just barely hear their soft-voiced exclamations of surprise.

"A first edition? Are you sure?"

"Imagine what it's worth!"

"What's the due date?"

"July twenty-fifth, 1947."

"Patience Hathaway."

"Is that . . . dried blood on the spine?"

All four librarians suddenly looked up and began to scan the people in the lobby. Alice pivoted quickly so that her back was to them. That's when she caught sight of Ivy. It wasn't Ivy as Alice had always known her. Ivy was fully *there*, her outline crisp and clean, every color vibrant. Her plaid jacket was a beautiful blue and gold. Her dark brown ringlets danced up and down as she tossed her head. Her gloves were crisp and white, and her valise was clearly brand-new—the perfect accessory for a little girl traveling for the first time. She looked just like a real, live six-year-old.

Ivy giggled and spun around, so pleased to show off her traveling clothes. "I'm so excited! I'm going on a trip!"

"But, Ivy," said Alice desperately, "I have to tell you something!"

"I know, I know," said Ivy. "I love you, too!"

Ivy's solid form began to sparkle, as if every molecule of her body had turned to glitter. She grew brighter and brighter, and then in a *poof,* the tiny pieces of her rained down and disappeared. The sound of jingling bells filled Alice's ears and then faded for the last time.

"This is *by far* the most overdue book we've ever had returned to the library!" said the voice of the director.

Alice sat down on one of the armchairs in the lobby. Her legs could no longer hold her up. She sank her head into her hands, her heart heavy in her chest, and she began to cry.

Chapter 20

Alice did not return to the House for the rest of the day. She stayed away the next day, too.

But on the day before the demolition, she found herself unable to ignore Ivy's final words. It was Sunday, a day of grace. Her parents were both sleeping, so Alice picked up her canvas tool bag and slipped outside.

When she entered the House and closed the back door behind her, she noticed the profound quiet. It was the kind of quiet that enters your bones and settles there, making you wonder if the earth itself has stopped spinning on its axis. Alice loved this kind of quiet, even when it made her sad, as it did this morning.

She looked into the front parlor and felt proud of the work she'd done. It was a job worthy of the Cannoli and Potchnik families. She thought of her ancestors on both sides, who had handed down the necessary skills, innate abilities, and important life lessons that had made it possible for her to fix what had been broken. Great-Great-Grandfather Alessandro Cannoli had stowed away on a ship at the age of fifteen and given Alice a taste for adventure. Great-Great-Great-Uncle Ivan Potchnik had stared down the czar's troops as they advanced on his tiny village and shown Alice how to be brave. And Grandmother Cannoli, who could shoot a quarter out of the sky, even when the sun was shining right in her eyes, had taught Alice the importance of seeing what others couldn't see. There were so many more. In her heart, Alice felt a deep sense of gratitude for all they'd given her.

She placed her tool bag on the floor by the archway and allowed herself time to admire it all. The parlor was beautiful, just as it had been when the House was born. The smooth wooden floors gleamed. The chandelier sparkled in the early morning light. The sofa with its beautiful satin cushions looked as though someone had just been sitting on it and as though someone would return soon to sit there again. The entire room seemed to speak of lives once lived and lives still being lived.

Alice placed her palm on the heart tile of the fireplace. Was it her imagination, or was the tile cooler than the last time she'd put her hand there?

She stared up the long staircase to the second floor. It was such an elegant piece of craftsmanship, with its curved mahogany banister and delicately carved balustrades. She began to feel the familiar Potchnik Itch to start a new project.

But even Alice knew the staircase would never be restored. Tomorrow morning at seven o'clock, the House would be demolished by a wrecking ball. There was no time to save anything. No time.

Alice looked up the staircase and thought of Ivy's last words. She walked upstairs and entered the attic.

It was Sunday-morning quiet there, too. Early morning light dropped in through the window of the arched eyebrow dormer and landed lightly on the floor. The room was neat again: the broken glass from the floor lamp was gone, the bookcase set aright, and all the books returned to their shelves. There was no sign of the struggle that had taken place just two days earlier.

Alice knew she was not alone in the dim and silent room. She peered into the dark corners, waiting for her eyes to adjust to the lowered light. After a minute, she could just make out a subtle movement in the far corner where the attic ceiling sloped to its lowest point. Something was breathing, the heavy breath of a wounded animal that has retreated to a sheltered place to die.

"Are you okay?" asked Alice quietly, remembering her promise to Ivy. She took several steps closer.

There was no answer from the Fury. In the dim light, Alice

could see that it was a tangled mass of scribbles, no longer in the shape of a powerful and angry tornado. It had devolved into a heap on the floor. A lengthening trail trickled from the pile as if the Fury's essence was slowly draining.

"Are you hurt?" asked Alice. She took a few more steps and now could see that there were several trails of the Fury's essence seeping away.

"Oh!" said Alice, alarmed by the sight. She remembered what Ivy had said about a spirit's essence scattering and how the spirit spends all eternity looking for the lost pieces. *It is the worst fate of all*, Ivy had said.

Alice looked around the attic. It was the first time she had entered the House since Ivy had moved on. Everyone was gone. Danny, Mugwort, and Ivy, which had been the hardest to bear of all. There was no one to call for help.

"House?" whispered Alice. She knew there was no point in calling for the House. The House was all around. It was everywhere, and it heard everything, perhaps even her thoughts, but still she said it again to steady herself. "House?"

A pain—part electrical shock, part bone-cracking coldness—shot up her left leg. Alice looked down to see that a trail of the Fury's essence had pooled around her foot. A feeling of pins and needles was spreading up her leg, accompanied by a deep, deep numbing. Alice pulled her foot away and the feeling subsided, but the Fury continued to ooze its essence as its breathing slowed even more.

"You need help," said Alice. Something was broken, and

Alice needed to fix it. She looked around the attic for a tool she could use and caught sight of the broom and dustpan in the far corner of the room. Taking hold of the dustpan, she knelt on the floor. Careful to stay out of the way of the trails of essence, she used the dustpan to scrape the oozing matter back to the center of the pile. The liquid was thick like molasses. It slithered and seeped, but Alice *was* able to push some of it back to the middle.

She worked quickly, moving in a circle, scooping with the dustpan in a steady rhythm. Every time she managed to transfer some of the ooze to the center, more of it seeped out somewhere else. She felt like she was trying to push back a rising tide. Still, after ten times around the circle, Alice could see she was making some progress. For every scoopful of essence she returned to the Fury, about half of it dribbled back. Slowly, the pile was growing higher.

Alice worked for an hour. Her shoulders ached, her right arm felt like a rubber band, and her knees sent shooting pains up her legs. She wasn't sure how much longer she could continue, but she was caught in the Cannoli Compulsion: the inability to stop working on a project until it was finished. She labored on.

At last, she could see that the tangle of scribbled lines was beginning to churn in an organized fashion and that the trails of seeping essence were being pulled in without her help. Without a doubt, the Fury was beginning to reconstitute.

Alice stood up, her knees almost buckling beneath her, and

staggered back. She watched the growing energy of the Fury. The scribbles began to look like a flock of birds, flying in one direction and then swinging wildly in another. Coordinated chaos. As Alice watched, she was astonished to see a form begin to appear.

First, a tall column rose up, with the bottom half ballooning into a full-length skirt. Then arms flowed out of the middle, and finally a head took shape within the swirling mayhem of the frantic scribbles. The confused lines grew tighter and tighter, until—with a loud crack—all the disconnected bits joined into one and formed the figure of a young woman who looked as if she'd been drawn with a heavy charcoal pencil that never lifted from the page.

Alice stared at the woman's strong arms, stout middle, and thick hair pulled into a bun. The woman stared back at her. Their eyes locked. Alice leaped back with the shock of recognition.

"I know you!" she shouted. "You're a Potchnik!"

Chapter 21

"Mom! Dad!" shouted Alice, banging through the front door of the house and rushing for the stairs. Her parents were still asleep, but they sat up when Alice entered the bedroom. "Are the family photographs still in the basement?"

Professor Cannoli stretched her long arms up to the ceiling and yawned. "I'm afraid they are, my gingersnap."

Alice quickly located the box of photographs and returned to her parents' bedroom holding a picture frame in her hand. She climbed onto the bed and showed the photo to her parents. It was the same one she had asked her mother about just before the last lecture in the last house. "Who *are* these girls?"

Professor Cannoli looked at the photograph and smiled broadly. "The younger one is your great-great-great-great-aunt Pavlina! And the older one is your great-great-great-great-aunt Zoya!"

"The reason you exist!" said her father, circling his big bear arms around Alice and placing a kiss on top of her head.

"Yes," said Alice's mother. "As we told you, if it weren't for Zoya, your father and I would never have met."

"BUT WHO IS SHE?" demanded Alice, losing all her Potchnik patience and showing more than a usual amount of Cannoli crossness.

"To understand Zoya," said Alice's mother, "you must begin with the miraculous birth of Pavlina."

"It began with Pavlina," agreed her father, nodding his head.

"Pavlina was born on the night that soldiers descended on their tiny village. All the villagers fled to the woods to hide from the soldiers, but Zoya's mother *couldn't* because she was right in the middle of giving birth to Pavlina. Understandably, Zoya's father wouldn't leave his wife, and Zoya wouldn't leave her mother. She wanted to be the first person to see the baby, which she was certain was the little sister she'd always wanted."

"She stayed, with the soldiers coming? That sounds dangerous," said Alice.

"Oh, very! Madness, in fact, and the villagers were certain

the entire Potchnik family would be killed. *But!* It didn't turn out the way the villagers thought. The soldiers set fire to the *woods*, not to the houses, and many lives were lost, which is very sad."

"But not the Potchniks?" asked Alice, staring intently at the photograph.

"Zoya and Pavlina survived; their parents did not. And so Zoya, at the age of ten, became like a mother to baby Pavlina, and when Zoya was eighteen, they sailed aboard the *Adriatic* to America. Zoya had worked hard and sacrificed much to earn the money for their passage. She was *formidable* when she had made up her mind about something."

I know, thought Alice, touching the bump on the side of her head.

"The very first Potchniks to come to America!" said Alice's father. "Zoya is the founder of the Potchnik clan!"

"She was strong," said Alice's mother. "And brave and clever and determined and fiercely protective of her little sister."

"She was also the life of every party," said Alice's father. "She played the harmonica beautifully, and she received seven marriage proposals before leaving the village. She turned them all down because she wanted Pavlina to grow up in the land of opportunity."

Alice stared at her father. Could it be true? The Fury had played the harmonica?

"It's true," said her mother, as if reading her mind. "She was much sought after on account of her sharp wit, good spirits, wood-chopping prowess, and extraordinary cooking skills. She could have married any eligible man in the village, but she wanted Pavlina to have an education and a happy life."

"She was a good sister," said Alice.

"The very best," said her father.

"What happened?" Alice was almost afraid to hear the rest of the story. It could not end well.

"There are several conflicting versions on how they came to settle in this town," said Professor Cannoli, "but as none of them can be confirmed by primary *or* secondary sources, we will not indulge in unscholarly speculation. We do know that they arrived here in 1911, the same year the college was founded. Zoya had dreams of Pavlina becoming a student and then a teacher. Perhaps it was the new college that brought them here. In any case, Zoya went to work in the house of a wealthy family."

. . . in the house of a wealthy family . . .

Alice pondered that phrase and the casual way her mother said it. Her mother was telling a story that lacked *context*. If her mother had known that the "house of the wealthy family" was in fact the house next door—would that phrase have gained the weight and importance that it deserved? There was a House, and in that House whole lives were lived. And there was happiness and tragedy and joy and sorrow. It was so much more than the "house of a wealthy family." It was a home. If

Alice had told her parents everything—all of it—would her mother have said, "How incredible!" and would her father have said, "What a thing!" Or would they have looked at her with doubt in their eyes? They had never doubted her before, but Alice knew, as all growing children do, that there's a first time for everything.

"Then what?" asked Alice.

"Zoya was hired as the household cook, *and* she persuaded the family to allow Pavlina to sleep in the servants' quarters. Pavlina attended school in the day and worked for free as a scullery maid in the afternoons and evenings. Servants were never allowed to bring family members into a house of employment, but Zoya persuaded them by agreeing to work seven days a week without a single day off."

"She was one in a million," said her father. "Everyone in the family says so. There has never been a Potchnik as strong and determined as my great-great-great-aunt Zoya."

"But what *happened* to them?" demanded Alice, sensing a twist in the story. Ivy had told her of a great betrayal that had taken place in the House.

"It's really very sad," said Alice's father. "One of the few Potchnik tragedies. When Pavlina was sixteen, she fell in love with a boy who dreamed of traveling west. She wanted to marry him, but Zoya refused. She wanted Pavlina to go to the local college and become a teacher. They argued, but Pavlina wouldn't change her mind. So Zoya concocted an elaborate lie: She told the boy that Pavlina was in love with someone else and showed him proof of the fictitious romance. And she told Pavlina that the boy had died in a train accident and showed her proof of the made-up death. She also told Pavlina that the boy had been leaving town without her when he died so tragically."

"Zoya was very angry," whispered Alice. "Why else would she betray her sister like that?"

"Yes," said her mother. "And then she dropped dead."

"*What?*" asked Alice. "*She* dropped dead? Stories don't end like that!"

"This one does. She must have had a heart condition, something she didn't know about. We surmise it was hypertrophic cardiomyopathy, on account of her young age, seeming good health, and the suddenness of her death."

"Her heart was literally too big," said Alice's father. "She loved too much. And in the end, it was the death of her."

"But that's awful!" said Alice. Her parents nodded. "No! I mean it's *really* awful, because there's no way to make amends for Unfinished Business like that!"

"What do you mean?" asked Alice's mother with interest. Her father put one of his bear paws on top of her hand.

"What happened to Pavlina?" asked Alice urgently.

"She was devastated by the death of her sister, of course," said Alice's father. "But she married her young man, and he was a terrific guy. They moved to California, and Pavlina did go to college—state school—and became a teacher. They had a busy life with four children, but she still found time to learn to play the harmonica, in honor of her sister. Eventually, they brought most of the Potchnik family over, and that's how we came to this country."

Alice's mother tapped the photograph. "Pavlina kept this photograph on her night table until the day she died. Two sisters who loved each other very much."

"But she doesn't know!" wailed Alice. "She doesn't know that Pavlina had a happy life and that it was all thanks to her."

"Who doesn't know?"

"Zoya! She's a Captive!"

"A captive of what, Alice?" asked her mother.

"Of the House! Of her past! Of her anger!"

Alice's father looked at Alice's mother. "You did hear the part about Zoya being dead?" asked her father.

Alice scrambled out of the bed. "It doesn't mean as much as you think! I'll be back in a few minutes. We're running out of time!"

She hurried outside, doing her best to dodge the raindrops that pelted down on her. Even so, she arrived in the House with dripping hair and squishing shoes. "Sorry," she called out as she left muddy wet footprints on the staircase. But what did it matter? The House would be demolished tomorrow! The thought made her heart squeeze tight.

In the attic, Alice found the Fury cycloning about the room, swirling books and papers and small objects, disarranging everything she came in contact with. When Alice entered, the Fury paused, hovering in midair, her scribbles still racing madly in coils about her.

"Your name is Zoya," said Alice. "Did you know that?"

The Fury continued to churn, but more quietly.

"I can't help you," said Alice. "There's no way to make amends for your Unfinished Business. But I have news," said Alice, "and I hope it makes you glad. Pavlina lived a wonderful life—the best kind of life. She had a family and she became a teacher and her students adored her. She even learned to play the harmonica! She wasn't angry with you. She kept your photograph with her until the day she died. She knew you loved her. She always knew."

The Fury began to turn more slowly until finally she stopped spinning altogether. She hung in space, like an old-fashioned black-and-white photograph of a storm that happened a very long time ago. Then slowly, the bottom of the spiral began to unravel and fall to the floor. As the charcoal-black scribbles landed, they turned to a puddle of liquid silver. Alice could see her own face reflected back on the still surface, as we can always see traces of ourselves reflected back in the lives of our ancestors. Alice looked at the unmoving puddle and grieved. She grieved for this loss right now and for all the losses past— Danny and Mugwort and Ivy—and for the loss still to come. The House.

Alice, who was a rare old soul with more flint and steel in her small body than most people might have guessed, felt all these losses at once. She closed her eyes as tears began to slip silently down her cheeks. As they fell, they mixed with the pool of shimmering liquid silver, and the essence of Alice mixed with the essence of Zoya, Potchnik reunited with Potchnik.

When Alice opened her eyes, the pool of liquid on the floor was gone and hundreds of small stars, tiny pinpricks of light, swirled in the dusty air of the attic. The stars looked like a magical carousel all lit up, turning with music and laughter.

"Is it you?" asked Alice, and the stars twirled a little faster for an instant, as if a girl at a party was swishing her skirt in time to the music. "You're my great-great-great-*great*-aunt Zoya, and if it weren't for you, I wouldn't exist at all. Thank you!"

The stars spun up to the ceiling, gathering in a great constellation over Alice's head, and then they gently rained down on her, enclosing her in a swirling, glittering embrace. Alice turned slowly, looking at the beauty and light all around her, knowing that Zoya knew her. "I will always tell your story," whispered Alice. "I will tell it to everyone I know. You will never be forgotten."

The stars settled for a moment at Alice's feet, still turning in a slow circle as if the carousel ride were gently coming to an end. Alice and Zoya might have stayed like that for a time, enjoying each other's company, as family members do who have come together after a long separation. But the quiet of the early Sunday morning was disrupted by the loud grinding of metal gears, the distinctive beeping noise of a truck backing up, and the voices of people shouting instructions. The stars scattered and Alice ran to the dormer window to look out on the street below.

She had never seen one before, but the sight was unmistakable: a truck with an enormous crane and a wrecking ball was crawling down the empty street toward the House.

Chapter 22

"What are you doing?" shouted Alice, running through the rain toward the convoy of trucks.

"Stand back, little girl!" said one of the workers directing the big crane. "Steve, can you make sure she's behind the line?" He turned his attention back to the crane that lumbered down the street like a slow dinosaur foraging for food. Behind the crane were two large excavators and a squabble of pickup trucks.

"C'mon, kiddo," said a man in a hard hat and reflective vest. "You need to get behind the yellow tape. It's for your own safety." The entire yard had been encircled in bright yellow CAUTION tape, and men were placing wooden barriers in the road to prevent cars from entering the cul-de-sac.

"It's Sunday!" said Alice. "You can't do this!"

"We do a lot of big demos on Sundays," said the man. "It's better when there aren't people around. Safer. Although this rain isn't helping any. If you want to lodge a complaint, you have to take it up with Jerry," he said, pointing to the man that Alice had first approached.

"But you aren't supposed to start until tomorrow," said Alice.

Steve shrugged, shooing her back behind the yellow tape. "What can I say? This is what's on our schedule."

"You can't tear this house down!" said Alice. "It's full of things that need to be saved."

Steve threw up his hands. "I'm with you!" he said. "If it were up to me, we'd do a manual demolition and recycle everything. But that costs three times as much."

Alice was walking backwards as she pleaded with Steve when she slipped in some mud and stumbled onto the wooden sign. The International House of Dereliction. "Wait!" said Alice, holding on to the sign. "Can you at least save this sign for me? I live right next door. That house. It would mean a lot!" Her hope was that pulling out the sign and transporting it to her yard would buy her a few extra minutes inside the House.

Steve looked back and forth from the sign to the Cannoli-Potchnik house. "Yeah," he said. "We can just pull that outta the ground with the excavator and drop it in your yard. But if it busts to pieces, there's nothing I can do about it."

"Thank you!" said Alice.

"Sure, kid. Just stay on the other side of the tape." Steve was already calling out to another worker. "Hey! Is the back of the house secure yet?"

Alice waited until no one was looking, then slipped behind a hedge and crept along until she was nearly at the House's back door. A worker there had just finished nailing the door shut and was now attaching a KEEP OUT sign. Other workers were boarding over the first-floor windows. They didn't want anyone wandering in by mistake.

When the crew had gone back to the front yard, Alice sneaked to the wooden bulkhead and slid down the dirty coal chute, landing on all fours on the basement floor. For a moment, she closed her eyes and felt the House around her, the subtle presence of its care for her. *This is what a home feels like*, she thought, truly understanding something that had eluded her for the first ten years of her life. She was determined that even if the House was demolished, the feeling of home would survive. "I don't have a plan," Alice whispered, "but I'm thinking."

Through her feet, Alice could feel the faint heartbeat of the House.

A heartbeat. A steady heart.

The heart. The heart tile.

Alice's eyes flew open. The heart tile. It was an original piece. It had been part of the House when the House was first built. It had been warm beneath Alice's open palm.

Alice hurried upstairs and rummaged through her tool bag, which she'd left under the archway. Peeking out one of the windows, she could see that the crane had become stuck in the mud on the front lawn. *Good.* She set to work.

The single most important part of removing a tile intact is to take your time. *If you rush*, Alice's father had often warned her, *the tile will snap in two, and then it's beyond salvage.* The trick, she knew, was to tap slowly with her hammer on the chisel, carefully chipping away at the grout until the tile popped out, all in one piece.

There would be no second chances.

Alice concentrated intently on her work, both because she needed to do the job right and because it helped block out her thoughts. The doors and windows had all been nailed shut, and the building was presumed empty. If the House collapsed, no one would even think of looking for a ten-year-old girl amid the rubble.

Alice continued to tap away at the grout. She was making slow progress.

There was another distracting thought that threatened to break her concentration. Zoya was still in the attic, and Alice didn't know if the spirit knew that the House was about to be demolished. Was it better if she didn't know? Zoya was a Captive and nothing could change that. She could *not* leave the House.

Alice heard a *thump* that came from the attic, and then two more, as if Zoya were tapping out a distress signal in Morse code. Alice put down her tools and hurried upstairs. She needed to at least explain to Zoya what was about to happen. The heart tile would have to wait. The House would have to stand strong.

In the attic, the stars were agitated, moving erratically and exploding before re-forming themselves into restless pinpricks of light.

"I have to tell you something," said Alice. "The House is about to be demolished. The trucks are outside now. Any minute, a wrecking ball is going to smash through the walls."

The lights hung still in the air as Alice spoke.

"I wish there was something I could do, but I can't think of anything. Ivy said you were different from all the other spirits. My parents said you were different from all the other humans. Maybe there's something *you* can do?"

The sparkles floated closer to the fireplace.

"Ivy said that you gain strength from stone," said Alice. "Try to gain your strength. Try! It might help you in some way. Remember who you are. You are Zoya Potchnik, the founder of the Potchnik clan. You took care of your sister Pavlina from the day she was born. You outwitted the soldiers and you managed to get to America. You built a good life. You gave Pavlina an education, and she became a teacher because of you. And my father met my mother because of you. And I exist because of you."

The twinkling orbs of light began to swirl in one direction.

They moved faster and faster until they became a single flash of light that swooped down the chimney. Alice heard a whooshing noise that sounded as if it traveled all the way to the basement.

She stared at the empty attic. For better or worse, Zoya knew the truth. There was nothing more Alice could do. She returned to her work in the parlor.

As she chipped carefully at the grout around the tile, she thought of what would happen to her if a wrecking ball came smashing through the wall before she had retrieved the heart tile. She supposed she would die. She was glad she had told her parents many times that she loved them.

But then, suddenly, she thought of the book. The architecture book from the library.

The one that was overdue and hidden so well under the front steps of her house that it would never be found.

Alice began to chip away at the tile faster.

Chapter 23

"Alice!" shouted a voice.

Alice jumped. Who knew she was here?

She heard banging at the back door and a familiar family curse: "Holy Cannoli!"

Alice lowered her chisel. "Dad?" She dropped her tools and ran down the hallway to the back door, where she could hear her father pounding on the other side.

"Dad, it's me! How did you know I was here?"

"I followed your footprints in the mud!"

"Don't worry, Dad, I'm fine! I just have to finish something and then I'll be right out. I promise!"

"Finish something? No! Alice!" Her father's voice was

panicked. She had never heard him sound like this before. "You have to come out *right now*. Your mother is arguing ferociously with the foreman, but he thinks she's a nut from the Historic Preservation Society staging a one-woman protest."

Alice could hear the low rumble of heavy machinery advancing on the House.

"I can't leave, Dad!"

Alice heard a tremendous thud against the door. In all her life, she had never known anything that could stand up to the determined weight of her father. "This door won't budge!" he shouted, adding an additional curse that was *not* one that belonged to the family. "How did you get *in* there?"

"I slid down the coal chute."

"Then how are you going to get out?" he shouted.

"I—" Alice hadn't thought about that at all. There was no way she could climb *up* the coal chute. A sudden realization came upon her: She was nailed inside the House like a corpse in a coffin. *And* she had an overdue library book.

Outside, an engine roared.

"Dad! I have to save the heart tile from the fireplace! I don't have time to explain."

"Alice, I'm coming in!" shouted her father.

Alice ran back to the front parlor, steadied her hands, and began delicately tapping the bottom edge of the tile, as if she had done this a hundred times before. As if she had all the time in the world. As if a ten-thousand-pound wrecking ball wasn't about to come swinging through the front wall of the house.

Concentrate, she told herself. *Trust your hands.* Her father had said these same words to her many times over the years. The words and the wisdom they contained were a part of her, like her skin and muscle and bone. She tapped at the tile. If she could just block out everything else that was going on . . .

"Alice!" Her father came running down the hallway and into the foyer. The sudden noise of his appearance caused Alice to miss the chisel completely. The head of her hammer came down sharply on the tile next to the heart tile, cracking it in two.

"Adam's ale!" cursed Alice, as she turned to look at her father and saw that he was covered in coal dust. "Dad! You came down the coal chute?"

"It was a tight fit, but gravity helped! Alice, we have to go *now*. We can't—" He stopped, suddenly seeing the room. His expert eyes took in the luster of the floor, the restored plasterwork, the glinting chandelier. "Did you do all this work?" he asked, his eyes landing on the perfectly restored fireplace.

"I was going to show you and Mom. But things kept *happening* . . . I didn't mean to turn it into a secret." Alice wondered if her parents would ever trust her again.

"What a marvel you are," whispered her father, and Alice burned with pride.

Outside, the rumbling of the trucks grew louder.

"We really do have to get out of here," said her father. "Your mother is a force of nature and could probably prevent the sun from rising, but they're paying those workers double time and that foreman isn't going to wait forever. Let's go!"

"I need to take this tile with me," said Alice, returning her attention to the fireplace.

"Why?" asked her father. "It's just a tile!"

"It's not. It's the heart of a home," said Alice, "and I'm not going without it."

Just then the wrecking ball smashed into the front façade of the House. The impact threw Alice to the floor, and her father crouched over her, using his bearish arms and wide torso to protect her from flying debris.

"No time to lose!" said Alice's father, pulling Alice up off the floor. "What do you need me to do?"

"I'll work on the tile. You find a way out of here."

Alice's hands were shaking as she tried to steady the chisel. Before she could begin her gentle tapping, the wrecking ball smashed into the House again. This time, the northeast corner crumbled and part of the second floor fell through. Alice could hear a cheer from the workmen in the front yard. She could also hear her mother's voice shouting things Alice had never heard her mother say before.

"Alice!" said her father, rushing back to the parlor. "Are you all right?"

"Yes! Keep looking for a way out! We're going to need it *soon*!" Alice continued to tap delicately at the tile. She felt like a heart surgeon performing an operation in the middle of a battlefield.

"Everything's nailed shut! I'm going upstairs to see if we can climb out onto a tree." When his foot touched the first step, a howling wind poured down from the second story, pushing him back and sending him sprawling onto the foyer floor.

"What is *that*?" shouted her father as the air continued to swirl around him.

"I can't even begin to explain," shouted Alice over the roar of the wind. More than ever, she needed to focus on the heart tile. *Tap. Tap. Tap.*

"Alice, we have to go NOW!"

"Dad, I got it!" The tile was in her hand, released from the grouting, released from the House. "Let's go!"

She stood up just as the wrecking ball smashed into the House for a third time. But now that the wind was fully unleashed inside the House, it pushed against the destructive pressure, equalizing the two forces so that the wrecking ball almost bounced off the façade without leaving a dent.

"Can you feel it?" shouted her father above the crashing noise. "The air pressure? This isn't right."

It's trying to push something out, thought Alice. But what? She already had the heart tile in her hand. What else needed to be saved? "We have to get downstairs," she said to her father.

A scream tumbled down the staircase. It startled Alice so much that she tripped, and the heart tile flew into the air.

"Dad!" shouted Alice. Her father turned, and with the dexterity of a Potchnik, leaped and caught the tile with both hands.

Alice took the tile from him and tucked it into her shirt.

They made it to the basement just as the wrecking ball landed a direct blow on the western wall of the House.

"This house can't hold on much longer," said her father.

They scrambled into the coal bin and stared at the open sky above them.

"We have to get up the coal chute," said Alice. "We need something to stand on."

"Hang on, Alice," said her father. "Let me get you out first. Come on, up on my shoulders, like when you were little."

Her father crouched slightly, and Alice climbed up his broad back and onto his shoulders. He positioned them directly under the open chute.

"Okay," he said encouragingly. "On the count of three, you jump. One, two, *three*!"

Alice's father sprang to his full height as Alice rocketed herself off his shoulders. She sailed through the open door of the coal chute and somersaulted on the soft grass. Quickly, she checked the heart tile; it was still in one piece.

She peered down the chute. Her father had found a rickety wooden crate and placed it under the opening. Gingerly, he climbed on top of it.

"Give me your hand. I can pull!" said Alice.

Alice's father reached up and Alice braced herself against the stone foundation of the House. She knew there was no chance she could pull the impressive weight of her father out of the basement, but she was going to try. She had done a lot of things this past month that she never would have thought possible. Maybe she had one last miracle left in her. Maybe, like the House, she could draw strength out of stone.

"The pressure is building in here!" shouted her father. "The whole house feels like a balloon that's ready to pop!"

Alice wondered what the House was thinking. Did it want to explode itself before it allowed the wrecking ball to do the damage? Or was there something else at work? *What do you want?* she asked.

Her father struggled to climb up the slippery chute while Alice grasped his hands and pulled. Between the two of them, they managed to wedge her father in the narrow passageway. His feet dangled above the crate, and he was unable to move up or down.

"I'm stuck," said her father. "Well and truly." Alice could see that he wasn't exaggerating. He was like a cork in a bottle of champagne.

"You *can't* be, Dad," said Alice, tugging uselessly on one of his thick hairy arms. The windows of the House were beginning to bulge, as if the air pressure inside the House were climbing to a dangerous level. Meanwhile, the engine of the wrecking ball revved loudly, and Alice prepared for another assault, whispering to the House, "Please hold on. Please! He's my father."

"I feel like there's a tornado under my bum!" shouted her dad. "Really, Alice, I think the whole house is going to blow! Go to your mother!"

The roar of the truck quieted momentarily, and Alice could hear her mother shouting, as if from her podium, " . . . hereby and in the presence of all those gathered as witnesses to this *atrocity*, I am invoking my right of protest as a citizen of this country and a member of this neighborhood . . ." Then her voice was drowned out by the renewed roar of the engine. Clearly, Alice's mother hadn't been able to convince the foreman that there might be a ten-year-old girl inside the boarded-up house. She had switched to plan B and was following the well-worn path of civil disobedience.

"C'mon, Dad, this is it," said Alice, leaning over to pull with all her might. In a whisper, she added, "Listen to me, House. Please. This is it. *Help me.*"

The engine roared. Alice pulled on her father's arms. The stone walls of the House bulged out and then compressed in. The pressure was too much. Mr. Potchnik exploded out of the coal chute, sending both of them sailing through the air. They landed on the soft grass. As Alice looked up at the sky, she saw the chimney spew forth a thundercloud of soot and ashes. In the midst of it, Alice could see a constellation of stars shoot out of the chimney and arc across the sky. The stars disappeared down the chimney of the Cannoli-Potchnik house.

"Come on, Alice!" shouted her father, scrambling to his feet and grabbing his daughter's arm. "It's all coming down!"

And it did. The sudden and brutal force of the expansion and compression of the outer walls had proved too much for even a house that had been built so well and stood so long. The entire structure collapsed with the beauty and precision of a choreographed ballet. Even in destruction, the House was magnificent.

When the dust cleared, Alice could see that not one wall, not one post, not one beam was left standing. The House had done its job well. It was reduced to rubble.

Chapter 24

The fire burned brightly in the fireplace, drawing Alice closer to its warmth. She had just finished reading a letter written by her great-great-great-great-aunt Zoya, which Alice had tracked down by finding a distant cousin on the internet. For her new unschooling project, Alice had been researching Zoya's life. She had found old letters, a brief mention in a local newspaper, the ship's manifest that recorded her and Pavlina's entry to America, and even a half-filled diary that Alice had unearthed from the rubble of the House. It was surprising how many documents were left behind by a life that was so short and difficult.

Alice was planning to write a book, and with her mother's help, she hoped to get it published. The book would tell

Zoya's story, and if she told that story well, then people would read it and never forget who she was. She would always be a Past Due because she could never make amends for her Unfinished Business, but at least the House had made sure that her essence wouldn't be shattered for all eternity. She was safely housed in the Cannoli-Potchnik attic. Zoya would not become one of the Settled Ones, but Alice was determined she would never be a Forever Forgotten.

In the meantime, Alice and her father were busy renovating their "Forever House," which Professor Cannoli had been deeded as part of the renegotiation of her contract. As it turned out, a certain Professor Gurkenstein had bragged to the head of the Anthropology Department at the University of Minnesota that she had listened to the greatest lecturer alive. The head of the department had been intrigued enough to get on a plane so that she could observe Professor Cannoli in action.

The title of the lecture was "Multimodal Practices in Training Children to Defy Authority: A Fragmented Approach to Fracturing the Status Quo." The visiting head of the department was entranced. She offered Professor Cannoli a professorship on the spot, with such a large increase in salary that Professor Cannoli seriously considered taking the job.

When Dean Sheridan heard about the offer, she told Professor Cannoli flat out that she would do whatever it took to keep her at the small college. In addition, Alice, who was the only family member who knew that Zoya was now a Captive of their new house, created a seventy-two-slide lecture entitled

"An Anthropological Perspective on Staying Put: The Difference Between a House and a Home." At the end of the lecture, Professor Cannoli hugged Alice so hard that Alice fainted dead away and required multiple cold-water washcloths to bring her back to consciousness.

And that is how the wreck of a house they were living in became theirs to own and keep forever.

A bargain, thought Dean Sheridan.

A project! rejoiced Alice's dad.

A little more time, whispered Alice to Zoya.

The first repair job had been to give the heart tile pride of place in the living room. It glowed above the restored fireplace with its mahogany mantel and intricate carvings.

That night, Alice had gone to bed unusually weary after a hard day of heavy physical labor. She fell asleep immediately and dreamed she was in her family's house—and it was *this* very house she dreamed of. Once she dreamed the house was surrounded by an encampment of friendly soldiers who were keeping her safe. Once she dreamed she was outside in a gentle rain, and when she looked into a puddle on the sidewalk she saw Danny's face reflected back at her. And once she dreamed that she was wearing blue-striped pajamas, and she was saying good night to the moon and the brush and the red balloon, but somehow all of them were really Ivy. She was in every object in the room, and she was in the house itself.

It seems that the House had finally brought Alice home.

Every day after that, Alice rested her hand on the tile and

felt the soothing, steady heartbeat of the House. It gave her a feeling of hope, just as it had done on that first day so long ago.

One evening, almost three months after the House had been demolished, Alice settled on the couch between her mother and father. Her mother was reviewing notes for a lecture she planned to give the next day entitled "The Significance, Historical and Practical, of Identifying and Eliminating Spoiled Milk Before It Is Accidentally Consumed," which was to be given to an enthusiastic audience of two. Her father was poring over a catalog in search of a sculptured finial to match those that decorated the gables of the roof.

Alice was thinking through another unschooling project she hoped to begin soon. She wanted to create a way to talk with Zoya, so that one day Zoya could tell her own story. It would be a tricky piece of linguistic magic to figure out how to talk to a thousand pinpoints of light, but Alice had hope. And she was glad that Zoya no longer needed to take the shape of an angry, scribbled tornado. In her own way, she was Settled—a peaceful gathering of lights that held her essence.

The podium glowed in the firelight, seeming to beckon lecturers of all kinds—anyone who had something to say and the courage to stand up and say it. Alice imagined herself someday standing at a podium like this one, with her own thoughts and her own words to share.

Perhaps she would give lectures about things that exist outside the realm of the physical world.

Perhaps she would take things that were broken and make them like new.

She was a Cannoli-Potchnik, which meant that she was capable of anything in *this* world and beyond. She had years ahead of her to become who she was.

Time would tell.